The Fox and the Camellias

Books by Ignazio Silone

THE FOX AND THE CAMELLIAS
FONTAMARA
THE SECRET OF LUCA
A HANDFUL OF BLACKBERRIES
AND HE HID HIMSELF
THE SEED BENEATH THE SNOW
THE SCHOOL FOR DICTATORS
BREAD AND WINE
MR. ARISTOTLE

The Fox and the Camellia

TRANSLATED FROM THE ITALIA

Ignazio Silone

Y ERIC MOSBACHER

HARPER & BROTHERS

PUBLISHERS

NEW YORK

To my friend Marcel Fleischmann

The Fox and the Camellias

one From the covered arcade that gave onto the garden Filomena called her husband several times, but in an obviously halfhearted manner. She was certain that he had heard her, though there was no reply, and she hurried back into the house.

"He won't be long," she said to a demure little woman who was standing diffidently in the middle of the room. "Meanwhile, why don't you sit down, Nunziatina?"

"I don't want to disturb you," the woman muttered in a thin little voice. "Won't you let me help you while I'm waiting?"

"Have a glass of our new wine instead," said Filomena, opening a cupboard.

The mistress of the house was an old lady whose expression suggested sadness and suffering. Nunziatina had already noticed that her eyes were red.

"Is anything the matter, madam?" she plucked up courage to ask.

1

Filomena sighed, and made a gesture of resignation.

"It's very quiet here," Nunziatina went on, looking out of the window. "Very quiet!"

"Quiet?" Filomena exclaimed in surprise.

The only sound to be heard was the rare hum of a car on its way toward the frontier. The river mist that had lain stagnant over the plain all the morning was now slowly mounting the valleys, leaving still visible a pale, tepid sun and slowly revealing, like a rising curtain, the dark gray neighboring villages, the green-tinted hills, the amphitheater of mountains, their tops still covered with snow. For the peasants it was still the dead season, and the fields were deserted; but the first periwinkles and one or two violets had appeared in the hedgerows and in the sunniest spots along the stream. Filomena had opened wide the windows of the old house. The porch was full of farm implements. A tiny lizard, perhaps the first of the season, was anxiously climbing the façade of the house, attracted by the yellow spikes of maize hanging under the arches of the arcade.

When he heard his wife calling, Daniele, accompanied by Agostino, was attending the delivery of a sow. He was tense and anxious. He had told his family he was not to be disturbed on any account so he did not answer.

"Shall I go and see what's the matter?" said Agostino.

"Stay here," said Daniele, with a grimace of annoyance.

Though he had taken all the usual precautions during the past twenty-four hours, he seemed very unsure of himself. These are always anxious occasions for any peasant, so that was not surprising.

But last year a sow of Daniele's had been seized with paralysis of the hindquarters, and its milk had dried up, and it had had to be slaughtered. This was an exceedingly unpleasant memory for Daniele, not only because of the loss, but because neighboring peasants, as well as some distant relatives, had again used the opportunity to rub in his lack of experience.

"At Schaffhausen you worked at a lathe," they said to him. "What on earth did you come back for?"

Unfortunately his neighbors never missed an opportunity of spiting him. The ill feeling was of long standing; his contemporaries still remembered how even in boyhood he had preferred the company of Italian refugees from over the border to that of young peasants and artisans of his own kind. These refugees used to arrive periodically in flocks, rather like swallows in the spring, no matter what government was in power, to escape the violent suppression that followed the economic and political agitation of the "reds." Some extreme and certainly immature ideas that young Daniele had about churches, armies and institutions in general were certainly an echo of his early friendships. Because of these, and certainly not because he was an idler, his father Ludovico did not spare his only son whippings of the kind that he gave recalcitrant colts. But it was wasted violence; his father never succeeded in making him give up associating with these foreigners and imbibing their unorthodox ideas. This failure exasperated him beyond all measure. Ludovico was an old-fashioned farmer, of a kind of whom few survived. Though rich and advanced in years, he spared himself nothing. He was on his farm every day except Sunday from dawn to sunset, and he took pride in sharing in the heaviest work. Anything other than this severe self-discipline seemed to him vice and disorder; and he could not resign himself to Daniele's revolt.

Some said that the young rebel found some comfort from the paternal fury with his mother, the gentle and kindhearted Signora Silvia, who was an Italian, the granddaughter of an exiled member of the First International. Her grandfather was a cult in her family, and she was brought up in a spirit of theoretical hero worship of all rebels against the established order, though by nature she was shy and retiring and detested any kind of commotion.

There was therefore nothing surprising in the pride she took in her son, whom she watched growing up into a strong, rough man like his father, from whom he nevertheless differed so strangely and so precociously. She considered the generous, warmhearted, unprejudiced Daniele a compensation sent by fate for all her trials, and lavished on him all her maternal tenderness, but unostentatiously, to avoid provoking his father.

No one ever had anything to say against Signora Silvia. Because of her delicate health and retiring disposition she spent nearly all her time indoors; and, when she took one of her rare walks along the farm paths near the house for the sake of a little fresh air, she would generally be accompanied by one of her daughters. She had no aptitude for housework or gardening, perhaps because she had never done these things as a girl. Sometimes she tried mending, but she was apt to prick herself with the needle and burst into tears, and she could not tell the difference between an onion and a dahlia tuber. When she was not looking after her daughters, she spent her time reading; books were her overriding and inexhaustible passion. She read with interest anything she could lay her hands on, but had a special predilection for travel stories and biographies; and, when she had nothing new to read, she reread her old favorites. Unfortunately for the peaceful life of the family, this passion of hers became the principal subject of dissension between her and her husband, or at any rate the pretext and excuse for his outbursts. Ludovico had known all about her taste for books and daydreaming during their engagement, and at that time used actually to boast about them. "I want my wife to be a lady, not a domestic servant," he always said. The first few years of their married life passed off happily enough, but then the farm lost money for several years, because of hailstorms and an outbreak of aphtha among the cows, and his temper got worse and worse. He started regarding her gentleness as hypocrisy and weakness, he took her shyness for cowardice and when he surprised her with a book it was enough to send him into a fury.

His outbursts grew more and more violent. They often took place when he came home from work, sweating, dirty and tired, and found his wife under the arcade or lying on a couch in the sitting room, depending on the time of year, immersed in a book and apparently aloof from the trials and tribulations of those about her. Anyone who witnessed one of these scenes might easily have been tempted to take his side. But, whatever the rights and wrongs of the situation, he put himself in the wrong by the way in which he gave vent to his feelings. He soon got to the point of denouncing and deriding his wife in the children's presence, calling her an idler, a dreamer, and a parasite; and to prevent her from getting new books he ended by descending to the meanest expedients; he gave her no money for her own use, and ordered the postman to hand to him personally all parcels addressed to any member of the family. But the success of these stratagems was short-lived. In one way or another she still managed to get books, whether from the public libraries or by exchanging old books for new at the bookshops; and she did so smoothly, swiftly and unobtrusively. But Ludovico was not a man to accept defeat in his own house.

The poor woman's only defense against his growing rages was the quality of the books she read.

"You can see for yourself," she would say, "I never read anything vulgar or indecent."

But, in Ludovico's opinion, even the most innocent reading was dissolute and depraved. He believed it to be the duty of every good Christian, and of every good Christian woman in particular, to try and suppress his or her imagination, in view of the unfortunate impossibility of clipping its wings like a pigeon's. Imagination, he used to say, was a bait and a lure which tended to give

6

women, even women who were shut up in the house day and night, frivolous and whorish ideas. The good man's argument was as pathetic as it was unoriginal.

Their two daughters were torn between secret agreement with their father and piety toward their mother, and their only way of reacting to the frequent scenes between their parents was with tears. But Daniele, who grew up into a young man no less forceful in nature than his now aged father, had to struggle to prevent himself from committing violence against him.

One day, when she was alone with her husband, Signora Silvia plucked up courage to say to him:

"You ought not to talk to me like that in front of Daniele."

"Why on earth not?" he asked curiously.

"It's hard to explain," she murmured. "But perhaps it might be wiser."

"You mean he might take your side?" said Ludovico with a sneer.

"Well, not mine personally, but his mother's," she said apologetically.

"Well, let him try!" Ludovico said defiantly.

Thus poor Signora Silvia lived in constant fear that one day Daniele's temper might get the better of him, and whenever she was alone with him she preached at him the virtues of self-control.

"Don't forget he's your father," she would say. "If you really love me, try to be patient and keep your temper."

It was actually his awareness of the collusion between

7

mother and son, of a bond between them strong enough to impose restraint on a nature as violent and in some ways as ungovernable as his own, that exasperated Ludovico most of all; and added to it was the suspicion that Daniele was not unconnected with his mother's secret supply of reading matter. But for this, he would probably never have caused a scene as painful as that which took place in front of the whole family one winter evening.

Nothing special had happened during the day. In the afternoon some snow had fallen, and it had got dark earlier than usual. A great silence hung over the whole countryside. After dinner Ludovico went upstairs, just to tidy up a bit, he said; and his wife and children waited for him, sitting round the big fire of beech logs in the kitchen. Daniele had drawn a jug of new wine from the barrel—it was still rather cloudy and sweet, but good— and his sisters were roasting chestnuts over the fire in a pan riddled with holes like a sieve. Ludovico's heavy footsteps made it easy to follow his movements as he went from room to room overhead, and his family waited for him before pouring out the wine. He came down again unusually slowly and noisily, but only when he appeared in the kitchen did his family realize why: he was accompanied by a servant, who was helping him to carry two big boxes full of books and magazines.

"Go and get the rest," he ordered the servant.

His expression was impassive, but there was no doubt about his intentions.

"Tell me if by any chance there are any school books

among this rubbish," he said, turning to his daughters. "There's no hurry," he went on with a smile. "The nights are long, and we'll examine them one at a time!"

Signora Silvia, pale and terrified, watched the preparations for the auto-da-fé in silence, with her eyes fixed on Daniele's.

"Let's see what this one is," said Ludovico, picking up a book from the box nearest to him.

He read out the title slowly, almost syllable by syllable. "Giovanni Verga, *Mastro Don Gesualdo,* a novel." He put marked emphasis on the word "novel."

"Well, do you see?" he said with a sneer, looking round the room at everybody present. "Do you see what a Christian mother of a family reads? A novel!"

His appearance suddenly changed, and his apparent impassivity gave way to the rage that was boiling inside him. He flung the book violently into the flames, and Daniele sprang forward to rescue it. But his mother, who had not once taken her eyes off him, managed to seize him by the shoulder and hold him back.

"Please!" she implored him. "Please!"

Ludovico pretended not to have noticed this little scene, which was over in a flash. He was in no hurry; the ceremony he had thought out was only just beginning. Signora Silvia was trembling violently with emotion and the effort to restrain herself.

"Now let's have a look at another book," Ludovico went on, in an apparently detached tone of voice. "Let's see what other filth there is."

"Excuse me, Ludovico, I'm rather tired," his wife

9

interrupted, rising to her feet. "It must be the change of weather. Yes, it must be because of the snow! Excuse me if I go to bed. Give me your arm, please," she said to Daniele.

As soon as the two girls were alone with their father they burst into tears.

After that, because of the deterioration of her health, Signora Silvia withdrew to a room on the top floor, from which she never emerged. Her daughters and Daniele took it in turn to sit at her bedside. Her husband almost forgot her existence, and consequently her last few months were peaceful enough. "This has been the happiest time of my married life," she confided one day to her son.

But happiness rouses the envy of death.

There had never been any doubt in Ludovico's mind that as soon as his mother had gone Daniele would leave home. But he did not foresee that he would do so in a fashion so dramatic that it would stick in everybody's memory. Immediately after the return from the cemetery, while relatives and friends from neighboring villages were gathered at Ludovico's door, saying good-by to him and expressing their condolences, a servant came and told him that Daniele was preparing to leave; he had saddled a horse, and was filling a bag with things to take with him. The old man promptly left the sad company by which he was surrounded and hurried toward the stable, but halfway across the yard he only just managed to avoid being run down by the horse that Daniele had already whipped up to a gallop.

"Go to the devil!" the old man yelled after him. "But that horse is mine. Get down off that horse."

These remarks had no more effect than if they had been addressed to the horse's tail. The old man, blinded by anger, forgot all about the people still waiting for him outside his house and went straight to the gendarmery office to denounce his son for theft and have him brought back by the police, or at any rate to insist on the recovery of his horse. But, to his fury, things did not go according to plan. First of all, he had to wait a long time until the sergeant of gendarmery was found and persuaded to return to his office, for he too had been to the funeral and afterward, in accordance with custom, had sought comfort in a tavern. Then, when at last he did come back, the old man had to engage in a long and tedious argument with him about the appropriateness of taking such hasty action against his son, for the sergeant, particularly when he had been drinking, was a broad-minded and sensible man.

"But what would your wife say, just after she's arrived in heaven, bless her?" he said.

"Don't be a fool!" the old man answered. "Don't you realize that it'll be a lesson for her too?"

And so it went on until a message from Bellinzona put an end to the argument. Before taking the train for the other side of the St. Gotthard, Daniele had handed the horse over to a gendarme, who was already bringing it back to its master. Needless to say, this happy ending was not altogether to Ludovico's liking. The horse was important to him, of course, but less important than inflicting one last stinging humiliation on his son who, he believed, had now gone out of his life forever. The slight regret at the loss of his wife that he had felt— against his will so to speak, and more from the effect of contagion than anything else—during the funeral ceremony, and particularly at the graveside, promptly gave way to furious anger that same evening because of a discovery he made while helping his daughters to clear up the room which poor Silvia had occupied during the last months of her life. Under the bed he found a suitcase full of books and recent periodicals. The stream of oaths and curses that issued from his lips, while his daughters, weeping desperately, hurriedly shut the windows to prevent the neighbors from overhearing, provided an ugly ending to a day that had started quietly enough with the *requiem aeternam.*

As was to be expected, Daniele's spectacular flight became the subject of endless gossip among the neighbors. The parish priest actually preached about it, denouncing the sinfulness that lay behind the young man's insubordination, "his turning his back on the trials and tribulations of humble toil in the fields, his revolt of the senses, his yielding to the licentious mirage of city life." Ludovico was in church, and all through the sermon kept shaking his head in violent disagreement.

"No, no, no!" he said to the priest afterward when he met him in the churchyard. "You haven't understood Daniele at all; his case is different, and far worse; it's not rebellion of the body, but of the soul. It's madness!"

But the question that exercised the neighbors' minds

was: Whom would he leave the farm to?

They did not dare ask him outright, of course. After his son's shocking flight he became gloomier, more misanthropic, more intolerant than ever. A few young peasants who came and asked him for his elder daughter's hand were sent away with a flea in their ear. To spite the neighbors, and also to free himself from the two girls' continual sniveling, he ended by marrying them off that same year to two badly paid clerks at Bellinzona. After that his solitude was complete; he spent whole days without talking to a soul.

"But whom will he leave the farm to?" the neighbors kept asking.

He neither received nor sought news of Daniele, but the things he heard indirectly or from his daughters at first left him incredulous and then never ceased to surprise him.

Daniele, alone and a free man, did not take to the disorderly life that his father had foreseen. At first he went through some hard times, which he faced cheerfully enough, and then he settled down at Schaffhausen, with a well-paid job in an engineering shop, and there he stayed. At the same time a change seemed to take place in his character. He did not give up his friends, but he became much quieter and more reserved. It was difficult to say whether he also changed his views; he denied this, but perhaps only out of pride. At any rate he now disliked wasting his time in political wrangles, or "talk," as he contemptuously called it. In short, his behavior seemed to confirm the old saying: revolutionary at

13

twenty, conservative at thirty.

Thus it came as no surprise to those who knew him when he married a Ticinese girl whose family had long had a little restaurant at which Daniele generally took his meals. Ludovico was informed of the wedding by the girl's parents, who expressed their regret at their inability to invite him in view of his rupture with his son. Perhaps they hoped that their letter would lead to a change of heart on the old man's part; but Ludovico did not even answer, and Daniele was never told about it. In the course of time the bitterness of his feelings diminished, but he did not like talking about his father, or, indeed, about his childhood in general, and his wife Filomena soon resigned herself to this, as to his other peculiarities.

After a year's marriage a daughter was born to them, and Daniele named her after his mother, both because this was a very general custom and because he liked the name. However, as she grew up she developed a very different disposition. She was a slim, nervous, delicate creature, liable to fits of petulance. Even on her Sunday visits to her maternal grandparents, who lived at Schaffhausen, she did not conceal the fact that she was much less interested in them than in her paternal grandfather, about whom the family was forbidden to talk. This taboo never ceased to exercise her curiosity. She never lost a chance of asking questions, not only of her parents, who replied with grunts or generalities, but also of her aunts, to whom she used to write, as well as of everybody she knew who came from the Ticino, if she found out that they

14

came from the district where Ludovico's farm was. She seemed to have been born with this obsession.

One day she came home and told her father that the homework essay subject that she had been given was "my grandparents," and asked him what she should say about her grandfather Ludovico.

"Whatever you like," Daniele replied.

"Am I to tell the truth?" Silvia asked.

"Say what you know," her father said.

An exaggerated frown appeared on the girl's forehead.

"Shall I say that he threw you out of the house immediately after Granny's funeral?"

"Who told you that yarn?" said Daniele. Then he added: "He didn't throw me out, I went of my own accord. But there are some things you're too small to understand."

"But Mummy isn't too small, and she knows even less than I do," the girl promptly replied.

In spite of these troublesome questions, Daniele was fascinated by his elder daughter (a second daughter had been born a few years later), and he was immensely proud of her, and enjoyed playing with her and taking her for walks. When he was finally convinced that there was no escaping her insatiable thirst for knowledge, he decided that a rather more serious and even educative explanation of the difficulties of his youth and adolescence would be preferable to the gossip that circulated in the little Ticinese colony at Schaffhausen. So he tried to tell her about the almost patriarchal life of the old

15

families of the Ticino, particularly in the country, and about their rapid decline in recent years for reasons independent of anybody's will. In bad times people's characters easily deteriorated, he concluded. Silvia did not fully understand all that he said, and least of all could she see what it had to do with his relations with her grandparents. But she felt proud at her father's having given her his confidence and told her things he did not tell others, though obviously her curiosity was only partly satisfied, and not for very long.

A recurrent subject of her complaints was the holidays. Lots of her friends spent their holidays in the Ticino, and why shouldn't she, who had a grandpa there with a huge house and an enormous farm, even if he was a bad-tempered old gentleman? But that was a subject on which Daniele was obstinately deaf, though he sometimes mentioned it to his wife.

"I couldn't allow my father to suspect that I had any hankerings after his estate," he would say.

In the end chance played into Silvia's hands. Her school arranged a two-day outing to Locarno, to attend the Festival of the Camellias. The whole thing was under the strict supervision of the teachers, but girls with relatives in Locarno or the neighborhood were allowed a free afternoon. Silvia heard of this concession only after reaching the shores of Lake Maggiore, and it solved some of the difficulties of a plan that had been buzzing in her head throughout the trip. She knew enough about the whereabouts of her grandfather's house and farm to be unable to resist the temptation of going to see him, particularly as she could now do so without acting surreptitiously.

With rather ostentatious self-possession she made her way to the town square, where she hired a cab, which put her down at her destination after half an hour's trot. The farm gate was half open.

"Wait for me here," she ordered the cabman.

Her school uniform gave her unusual self-confidence. But, once past the gate, her courage failed her. Fortunately it was a holiday and the farmyard was deserted, so Silvia was able to stop and have a look round.

She was barely fourteen, but she had shot up quickly, and looked at least two years older; she was very attractive with her slender, agile figure, regular features, delicate complexion and the long, thick hair that fell about her shoulders. Slowly and cautiously she walked across the yard in the direction of the house. It looked something between villa and farmhouse. Everything was so quiet that, but for two open windows on the first floor and some washing hanging out to dry under the arcade, it might have been uninhabited. Silvia went on gingerly, looking back every now and then, and then suddenly stopped dead. Behind one of the columns of the arcade an old servant was lying on a seat, resting. His eyes were half shut, his white hair was untidy and his beard was several days old. He was wrapped in a long, dirty, discolored old dressing gown, and had a pair of worn slippers on his feet. To judge by the appearance of this servant, Grandpa must be in a bad way.

17

Silvia coughed to attract the old man's attention. He opened his eyes.

"Who are you?" he shouted angrily. "Where the devil did you spring from?"

The girl smiled to mollify him, and signed to him to talk more quietly.

"Is Signor Ludovico at home?" she asked softly.

"I don't know," the old man replied. Then he corrected himself. "Yes, he is at home. Why do you want to know?"

Silvia once more gave him a handsome smile, and went up to him and put a coin in his hand.

"That's all I can give you," she said apologetically, "because I've got to pay for the cab that's waiting for me at the gate."

For a moment or two the old man was speechless, his eyes darting backward and forward from the pretty girl to the silver coin that remained in his open hand.

"Why are you so interested in Signor Ludovico?" he asked in a gentler voice. "What do you want of him?"

The girl looked all round, and then said in a confidential whisper:

"I'm his granddaughter, Daniele's daughter, but I've come here secretly!"

The old man started, and rubbed his eyes as if to make sure he was not dreaming.

"Are you Silvia?" he asked, whispering this time too.

The girl nodded.

"Why did you say you came here secretly?"

"I came to Locarno with my school," she said. "My father wouldn't like it if he knew I was here."

"Will you tell him when you get back?"

"Of course!" the girl replied. "I don't have any secrets from him!"

"And will he beat you?"

"Oh, no!" Silvia said. "My father's a nice man, not a brute. But he won't like my having come here without his permission."

"Then why did you come? Did your mother suggest it?"

"She wouldn't dare!"

"Well then, why?"

"Well, I think it's obvious," the girl explained. "Signor Ludovico's my grandpa, isn't he? He seems to be a horrid old man, but he's still my grandpa, isn't he?"

The old man smiled.

"Your father . . ." he started, but did not finish the sentence. Instead he made a gesture as if to crush a fly, and then smiled again.

"Do you know you're very like your grandma?" he said. "She had the same name as you, and she was very pretty too when she was a girl!"

"So I've heard," the girl replied. "But they say I've inherited some horrid defects from my grandpa!"

"What defects?"

"I can be very obstinate and headstrong."

"Well," the servant exclaimed, "as for being obstinate and headstrong, your father—"

19

But Silvia had not much time to waste. "How is Grandpa?" she asked. "Has he got very old?"

"He's the same age as I am," the servant replied. "He's getting a bit stiff in the joints. And on top of it he's lonely, depressed, and has no one he can trust. But those are things that it's not very easy for little girls to understand."

He seemed to chew over the words before saying them.

"Well, I'll go and fetch him," he said suddenly, and made as if to get up. "He may be about a quarter of an hour, but not longer."

"No, don't go, I'm frightened!" exclaimed Silvia.

"Frightened of your grandfather?" the servant said in astonishment. Then he added, "You've no need to be frightened; he'll be delighted to meet you."

The old man struggled out of his seat—when he was on his feet he looked a giant—and hobbled off through the dark front doorway. Silvia was thrilled to the marrow; her plan was succeeding.

"Don't tell him I was frightened," she shouted after him.

She decided to take a stroll round the garden while she was waiting. The beds were carefully laid out. Though the house, to judge by the servant, was obviously neglected, the garden showed every sign of the most meticulous care and attention. When she looked round she noticed that light had appeared in the first-floor windows, and she spent a few moments looking up at them, perhaps expecting her grandfather to appear and call her. But a sudden noise behind the pergola caused her to hurry back under the arcade. There an even more unpleasant surprise awaited her: on the seat on which the servant had been lying there was a big, black dog with blazing eyes. She was seized with panic, and fled.

By the time Ludovico had taken off the tattered old dressing gown that had made his granddaughter mistake him for a broken-down servant and put on his best clothes, ready for a good laugh about his transformation, the girl had gone. He went out into the yard, walked round the garden several times and even made one or two forays into the farm, calling out "Silvia! Silvia!" every now and then. Finally, exhausted and disappointed, he decided he must have been dreaming. I'm going out of my mind, he said to himself. But in his wretched state even this alarming thought was a kind of relief. He went back to his seat and dropped off to sleep, thinking about his conversation with the strange apparition.

Next day a long letter of apology from the girl removed his doubts. But he too owed the girl an explanation, and he wrote to her at her home address.

When Daniele heard of Silvia's escapade, he naturally went into a towering rage. Then he decided, from what he could gather from his father's letter, that his daughter's behavior had not been devoid of a certain "dignity." In any case the ice was broken.

Not long afterward Ludovico wrote to his son. "I feel surrounded by carrion crows waiting to pounce on my corpse," he said. "Many greedy eyes are on the farm. I can't count on your sisters: they have always been snivelers, and their husbands are spineless clerks. But I have never had any doubts about your vigor and energy; and it seems that in the meantime you have straightened out your ideas. Better late than never. So I am willing to leave you the farm on condition that you undertake not to sell it and to come back and cultivate it yourself."

Daniele waited a month, and then his reply was exceedingly laconic. "I have thought it over," he said. "I accept." That was all. Ludovico, made suspicious by the long delay and the exaggerated brevity of the reply when it came, answered that naturally he would wish to give legal form to Daniele's undertaking. This time his son replied immediately. "My word is worth more than a legal document," he said. "If you don't trust me, leave your land to anyone you like."

His father sent him a telegram saying, "You're as insolent as ever." But he left him the land. At bottom Daniele was more like him than he had ever suspected.

With two men of that kind it was not surprising that knowledge of the agreement between them never came to the ears of any third party. And so, when Daniele reappeared on the scene to take possession of the house and farm after Ludovico's death, the neighbors felt cheated, and said it was a scandal.

It is rare for an urbanized ex-peasant to go back to the country. But, though he had been a good workman for so many years, Daniele had kept his peasant's hide—and something more than the hide. His tastes, and his way of speaking and laughing, still had the distinct country stamp. So his return to his birthplace, to working in the fields, to the environment of his youth, was an event that inevitably moved him deeply and filled him with melancholy, though he tried to hide his feelings from his family. He went back to waking at cockcrow, to looking at the weather first thing every morning as soon as he got up, and to recognizing the tracks of wild animals on the dust of the farm paths.

On one of the first walks he took with Silvia to show her the countryside, there was a sudden movement behind some bushes.

"It was a hare," he said with a laugh.

"Where? Did you see it?" the girl asked curiously.

"No, I didn't," he replied.

"Then how did you know it was a hare?" the girl wanted to know.

"I don't know," he replied, blushing.

Nevertheless all the neighbors considered him an intruder.

"Why did you come back?" was their invariable retort whenever he started grumbling about anything. "Weren't you better off in town?"

Daniele let them talk. He had less and less to do with them, and barely greeted them when they met, in spite of his sociable disposition, or perhaps because of it, in order to avoid quarreling. But the consequence was that, when he wanted a friend to talk to, he did not know where to turn. The laborers from over the frontier, of whom there were always plenty in that area, were all right for the heavy, dirty work, but he had to do all the difficult and responsible jobs himself.

two   Daniele did not confide to anybody, even his own family, the anxiety he felt about the delivery of his new sow. When the time came he consulted the vet, and stuck closely to his instructions. He had started the day before by withholding food from the animal, in spite of its grievous complaints, and giving it a dose of castor oil. But he needed someone to stand by and give him a hand. As he could not count on his wife and daughters for such crude and dirty work, or rather did not want to, he called in Agostino, a friend of his from Bergamo, who had for many years been settled in Switzerland like so many others from his part of the world. They had met and become friends at Schaffhausen, and had met again in the Ticino, though it was not clear whether Agostino was more attracted by friendship for Daniele or admiration for Silvia, his elder daughter. Perhaps it was a combination of both.

"How can Agostino help you?" Filomena said to her husband.

She did not like having Agostino about the house; he was an honest man, certainly, but he was ten years older than Silvia, had no money and was fond of drink. Moreover, Filomena had her own very definite ideas about Italian men who, she said, made gallant wooers but bad husbands.

"He's got a good pair of hands," said Daniele, trying to change the subject.

"But he's a bricklayer," Filomena insisted. "What does he know about animals? How can he help you?"

"It's true that he works as a bricklayer," said Daniele, "but he grew up in the country, and he's used to animals."

"Is that enough?" Filomena asked ironically.

"Perhaps it is," said Silvia. "Even wild animals obey a man who treats them fearlessly."

"Who's afraid of a sow?" exclaimed Filomena, annoyed at her daughter's interruption. "Nobody's afraid of a sow! But not everyone can help if it's in difficulties."

"The fact of the matter is that with Agostino there I feel more confident. I can't explain why," said Daniele.

That settled the matter, and Silvia threw her father a smile full of gratitude.

The delivery started well. Three little pigs emerged without difficulty, like three mice out of a wineskin. Agostino laughed and jumped for joy; he praised the sow for the unusual beauty of her progeny, using the phrases always used at every birth; and his principal preoccupation seemed to be to find an unusual name for each piglet.

"Be quiet," Daniele said to him. "We're not out of the woods yet."

The fourth little pig would not come out. The sow seemed exhausted. Lying on the straw, it was a huge mass of suffering flesh, a gray, warm, soft, quivering, complaining mass. The two men looked at each other, perplexed. Daniele was in a cold sweat. Should they let the animal rest? Might not delay be dangerous? Agostino took a water bottle full of *grappa* from a box on top of the pigsty and helped himself to a big gulp.

"You ought to have one too," he said.

"When it's over," Daniele replied, without taking his eyes off the suffering animal.

"I remember how a cow of my uncle's—" Agostino started.

"Hold her snout!" Daniele interrupted. He plunged his bare arm into the torn womb and drew forth the obstinate little pig, clearing the way for the rest. There were seven in all.

Daniele sighed with relief, and smiled for the first time that day.

"We've done it!" he said.

"We've done it!" said Agostino. "Not bad for a mechanic and a bricklayer. Now have a drink."

"We haven't finished yet," said Daniele.

While Agostino cleared away the dirty straw and cleaned up the floor, Daniele took the precautions necessary to protect the piglets from the risk of infection. He

27

was tired but happy; his movements were swift, calm and confident, almost affectionate. The neighbors would not have laughed if they could have seen him now. He laid the little animals side by side in a big box half full of clean straw, and covered them with a woolen blanket.

"Now let's go to the fountain and wash," he said at last.

"Do you know that Silvia asked me to dinner?" said Agostino. "Unless your wife . . ."

"For once you've earned it," said Daniele.

Silvia was sitting in the sun on a bench outside the front door with a demure little old woman, who was showing her with a needle and a piece of material how to make a buttonhole. When the two men approached, the woman rose respectfully to her feet.

"Silvia, we've done it!" Agostino announced with a laugh. "Just think, a mechanic and a bricklayer. Better than the vet."

"Bravo!" said the girl. "I expect now you're both thirsty." Then she went on: "Daddy, we've been waiting for you so as not to disturb you. Nunziatina wants to talk to you urgently."

"Couldn't she talk to your mother?" said Daniele.

"I don't know, but apparently not," said Silvia. Then she added, to make him realize how urgent it was: "She walked all the way here especially to see you. It took her more than an hour."

"If your mother isn't jealous, let's leave them alone,"

Agostino said to Silvia. "Come along, I'll show you the new arrivals. They're as beautiful as their mother and as intelligent as their father."

He took her by the hand and led her toward the box containing the newborn piglets.

When she was left alone with Daniele, Nunziatina had a moment of panic. She was a gray-haired little old woman, dressed in black, clean, neat, respectable, shy and easily frightened.

She too came from Italy, or more particularly from Florence, and had lived in the Ticino for about thirty years. She had been past her first youth when she arrived at Locarno to join a man whom she had trusted with all her savings. But he had lied to her, and left nothing but a false address. Pride or shame prevented her from confessing the deception to her penniless relatives and friends in Florence, so she resigned herself to living abroad, and alone. She was known as the little dressmaker, though she rarely made a whole dress; she earned the little she required for her simple needs by going to people's houses and doing simple alterations. Many better-off families in the neighborhood sent for her regularly. Perhaps they did so less for the sake of the work she did, which could easily have been done by others, than because they were sorry for her and liked her polite, ceremonious and totally unservile manners; and perhaps they liked even more the way she spoke Italian. Though for so many years she had heard nothing all about her but a dialect different from her own, she had preserved her Florentine speech intact, and it was full of charm. But, apart from her work, her life was sad, monotonous and lonely.

She plucked up courage and said:

"You know that I've always minded my own business, don't you?"

"So have I," Daniele brusquely interrupted her. "So if it's your business you've come to talk to me about, I'm not interested."

Nunziatina's eyes filled with tears.

"I'm sorry," she said. "In that case I won't trouble you any further."

And she made as if to go. But Daniele was touched by the humility in her voice and repented of his harshness.

"Well, as you've come such a long way," he said.

"As a matter of fact," Nunziatina went, with an almost childish tremor of the lips, "I don't really know whether it's my business or other people's. Will you be patient for a moment? Something has happened to me unlike anything that has ever happened to me before."

The two were standing under one of the arches of the arcade. The sun was setting, and a light breeze was springing up from the direction of the lake.

"Let's sit here," Daniele said. "Now tell me briefly what it's all about."

They sat on a wooden seat near the front door. Nunziatina thought for a moment, trying to pick up the thread of the speech that she had in mind.

"You know how many years I've lived in this neighborhood," she began. "When I first set foot in this house your mother, the dear unhappy Signora Silvia, was still alive."

She was trying to gain time.

"Please cut out the introduction and come to the point," said Daniele. "We know each other, don't we?"

Nunziatina's face contracted as if she were swallowing a difficult morsel.

"Yesterday afternoon," she began again, "I went to church as usual for the Adoration of the Sacrament. When I got home, my neighbor told me that a gentleman had called to see me. 'Did he leave a message?' I asked. 'No,' she said, 'it was just a visit.' 'A gentleman?' I said. 'A man? Didn't he leave his name?' 'He was a handsome man,' she said. 'If I understood him correctly, he was an old acquaintance of yours from Florence.' 'How old a man?' I said. 'What was he like?' 'A handsome man, dear, rather elderly. He promised to call again this evening,' she said. You know, of course, Signor Daniele, that I never have men visitors. My customers send their daughters for me, or leave a note for me at the dairy downstairs. Who could it have been? I can't tell you what a flutter I was in! I hurried down to buy some flowers and a little coffee and some biscuits, keeping my eye on the front door all the time, in case the gentleman came back. I was just moving the furniture in the sitting room when he did come back. He was a total stranger. He looked just like my neighbor said, an elderly gentleman, cheerful-looking and well dressed. As soon as he opened his mouth I could tell that he came from Tuscany; not from Florence, but from the country. 'I must talk to you,' he said. 'I have news for you from

Florence which I am sure will give you pleasure.' So I invited him in and asked him to sit down."

"Did he bring you news of your family?" asked Daniele, bored by the woman's verbosity. "Good news?"

"The gentleman's news concerned neither my relatives nor anyone I have ever met," Nunziatina replied. "He had nothing to say about Florence except about the sky line, the panorama, so to speak. In fact, it was nothing but a wretched excuse to get me to listen to him. I realized it just after I had said, 'I'll make you a cup of coffee,' and of course after that the saucepan remained in the sink. Well, he sat down and started talking to me about all the people I know here. 'You go to the houses of dozens and dozens of well-off people,' he said. 'How do you know?' I asked him. 'Do you live in these parts?' 'I know everything,' he replied with a smile that sent shudders down my spine. 'We know everything,' he went on, emphasizing each syllable; and on he went with his phony compliments. 'You hear hundreds and hundreds of conversations,' he said. 'Nobody's afraid of talking in front of you . . .' Don't be impatient, Signor Daniele, I've nearly finished. He went on talking to me as if I were a class of school children, all about love of our country and our duty to serve it. All that he said was fine and true, sacred even. 'But I'm not a recruit,' I pointed out, because what he said reminded me of a picture of young conscripts in my elementary-school book, with the caption: 'They go to serve their country.' I might easily have burst out laughing if I hadn't been so frightened by the way he spoke."

32

"Did he make you any proposition?" Daniele asked dryly.

Nunziatina ignored his brutal tone and answered simply:

"Yes, he even promised me money. So much a month. He said it might help to assure me of a serene and comfortable old age. Otherwise . . ."

"Did he threaten you?"

"He said that if I didn't do what they asked, they might refuse to renew my passport. Force me to go back to Florence."

"Well?" Daniele asked. "Did you accept?"

"Oh!" exclaimed the poor woman, more surprised than offended.

Daniele went on in a hard voice:

"Now tell me who sent you to me."

"No one!" Nunziatina protested. "Who could have sent me? I knew the way myself."

"Why didn't you go to other people you know?" Daniele insisted, with increased mistrust. "Why did you come all this way to see me?"

Nunziatina collapsed, without further resistance.

"I did go to other people," she murmured.

She was at the end of her tether; she lacked the strength for dissimulation. And why should she dissimulate? What did she have to hide? Suddenly she felt all the weariness and humiliation of that day spent going from house to house, scarcely touching food, after an almost sleepless night. It had been a monotonous calvary, going from door to door, appealing to people by whom she was generally better received. Each time she came to the end of her painful story and humbly asked for counsel, moral aid, friendly advice, in a flash she had seen smiling faces change expression, grow hard, assume a cold and suspicious look. In a few hours the whole tone of her life had changed. Gone were the politeness, the friendliness, even the touch of pity, with which she felt she was always received in the households which she visited. The poor woman was seized with dismay. She tried to withhold her tears, but could not; and she started sobbing, hiding her face in her hands. She barely succeeded in bringing out the words: "Excuse me!" She disliked weeping in front of strangers, not out of pride, but because she hated being a nuisance. Anguish shook her from head to foot, she was like a terror-stricken little girl. Daniele looked most annoyed at the scene, and did not know what to do.

"Come, come, calm yourself," he kept saying in an irritated voice. Then he made up his mind.

"I'll be back in a moment," he said.

He went and found Agostino and Silvia, who were laughing and running about under the vine trellis.

"Excuse me just a moment," he said to his daughter, and took Agostino aside.

The two men talked for several minutes, walking up and down. When Agostino went back to the girl, there was a worried look on his face.

"I'll come to dinner another time," he said. "This evening I'm busy."

"What are all these mysteries about?" Silvia protested.

three   The light in the girls' room had been out for some time when they heard the creaking of the front door for which they had been waiting.

"Did you hear?" Luisa whispered.

"Yes," said Silvia. "What's the time?"

Luisa put out her hand and switched on the bedside lamp.

"A quarter past three," she said, and turned out the light again.

"Where on earth can he have been at this time of night?" Silvia whispered.

"I expect he's got another woman," Luisa said with confidence. "All the men in this part of the world seem to need at least one other woman besides their wives."

"Who told you such nonsense?" said Silvia reprovingly. "I don't believe Daddy's got a dirty woman."

"She may be a clean one for all we know," replied

Luisa. "After all, he's a man like others. That's all I meant!"

"But didn't you notice that he went out in his working clothes and without shaving?" Silvia said.

"So you think men always shave first, do you?" Luisa replied. "And they take their clothes off, don't they?"

"Luisa, you ought to be ashamed of yourself, having such ideas at your age!" said Silvia in shocked tones.

But shame, like its opposite, comes only with age. Luisa had not yet reached it, but Silvia was now at the stage at which there were certain things that she did not dare talk about even to her father, from whom she used to have no secrets. Nowadays, if he said to her: "How are things between you and Agostino?," she would answer "All right," and change the subject.

"It's Mummy I'm surprised at," Luisa went on.

"I'm not in the least surprised," said Silvia. "She's obviously very fond of him."

"Yes, but like a servant girl," said Luisa. "Just like a sniveling servant girl! Doesn't it make you furious?"

"Try to go to sleep," said Silvia.

Some days of *Föhn* gave a sudden impetus to spring. The streams dashing down from the valley turned yellow and boisterous. Warm mists rose from the plain, which was cut in two by the straight ribbon of the canal. These were sleepless nights for nervous people, and for nature herself. The buds on the trees suddenly swelled and grew shiny, and the ditches and paths were lined with tender green.

Daniele decided to take advantage of one of these fine mornings to rid the vines on the trellis of the pest known locally as *gattina*. He brushed the stems with a wire brush to clear away the patches of blight and reveal the hidden chrysalises, and Silvia poured boiling water over them. The girl was unusually vivacious. She had put on a long, dark apron for the occasion, and had tied a red handkerchief round her neck.

Flocks of tiny sparrows were flying about among the trees, and some crows were hopping about on the grass, looking for worms. Here and there you could catch glimpses of the lake, which seemed a prolongation of the fields. An odor of reawakening earth hung in the air.

Silvia was tall and slim, but to reach the higher branches she had to stand on tiptoe and stretch. While doing so she caught her father looking at her admiringly.

"What's the matter with you?" she said.

"I'm not boasting," he said, "but you really are a very pretty girl."

"What?"

"A moment ago you looked just as if you were going to fly away."

"Really?"

"Would you really fly away?"

"Of course, but I'd come back in the evening."

"Like a tame dove."

The girl was delighted at the idea of being a dove, and several times she went through the motions of flying away. One of the reasons why she liked working with her father was that when she was with him there were always playful interludes, even during the most unpleasant jobs. Also, though they were so different in many ways, quite apart from the difference in age between them, her father always reminded her of Agostino. The extraordinary resemblances that she was always discovering between the two amused both of them, but convinced nobody, least of all Filomena.

"Haven't they got the same look?" Silvia would maintain.

"Rubbish!" her mother would say. "Your father's eyes are much lighter."

"I wasn't talking about the color of their eyes, but about their look," Silvia would insist.

As father and daughter were as thick as thieves and inseparable, and as Luisa, the younger girl, went to the secondary school at Locarno and so was away from home almost every day, Filomena was left to do all the housework by herself. But in the course of time she had got tired even of grumbling about this.

In one of her comings and goings between the kitchen and the trellis with a basin of boiling water, Silvia noticed a truck loaded with tiles draw up at the farm gate. The driver began hooting vigorously. She promptly recognized the man sitting beside him, put the basin down on the ground and ran toward her father, shouting, "Hurrah! Hurrah!" Meanwhile, Agostino jumped down from the truck to greet them.

"You must certainly be thirsty," the girl said to him. "Shall I go and fetch the bottle?"

"No, I'm in a hurry," said Agostino. "We're late with the truck."

His beard was several days old, as thick and smooth as the fleece of a sheep, but a dusty, earth-colored sheep.

"How's that business going?" Daniele asked him.

"There's a slight holdup at the moment, because the little dressmaker's ill," Agostino answered. "But it's nothing serious."

"Apart from that, is she willing?"

"I think so."

"Don't make her run any risks," said Daniele.

"Daddy," Silvia began as soon as Agostino had gone away, but her father interrupted her.

"Do you want to know what to do next?" he said. "That'll do with the boiling water. Pick up the diseased bits and burn them."

His daughter did as she was told. Daniele watched her hurry back to the pergola and start picking up the scrapings at the foot of the vine and putting them in a basket. She had had her twentieth birthday in November, and her father looked at her with pride and trepidation. A father is not slower than other men in recognizing and appreciating a daughter's attractiveness. Daniele found extraordinary the extent to which open-air life had in a short time removed some imperfections in Silvia that had been due to her overrapid growth, but had left the delicacy of her features unimpaired. Her golden-brown complexion was now in perfect harmony with her magnificent chestnut hair and her big bright eyes; and all her movements were full of grace. She was now like a fine, ripe fruit. But there was no doubt that she was the member of the family who had suffered most from the return

39

to the country, and that in her heart she must miss town life, the cinemas, the shops, the crowded streets which were clean underfoot even in winter. But Silvia never complained. She saw that her father often had obscure worries of his own, and she did not want to add to them.

When Daniele went back to the house to fetch a tool, he saw his wife at the farm gate in animated conversation with the neighbors. Filomena beckoned to him to join them. During the previous night a fox had raided some chicken runs at Cadenazzo and Robosacco. A woman was just saying that about twenty hens had been found which had bled to death with their throats slashed.

"If that was the case," an old peasant said, "it wasn't a fox, but a weasel."

"It was a fox!" another one said. "In one chicken run nothing was left but the feathers."

"You must do something," Filomena said turning to her husband. "We've had the fowl pest once, and a fox would be the last straw!"

"I'll set the trap," said Daniele.

"Do you think that's any good?" said the old peasant. "A fox is as cunning as the devil. Before touching the bait with his teeth he tests out the ground, and feels the meat with his paw, and draws it toward him, and . . ."

"Aren't traps any good, then?" said Daniele. "That's the first I've heard of it."

"That's because you lived in town," the old man said with a sarcastic smile. "The only foxes in town are in the furriers' shop windows."

There was some tittering behind Daniele's back, but

one of the peasants put things right again.

"You can't do without a trap," he said. "But it's just as well to scatter poison outside the chicken run as well."

"What's the good of that?" the old peasant said. "For a fox to waste its time gobbling up bits of meat scattered on the ground outside a chicken run, it would have to be not just starving, but weak in the head as well."

"It's often happened, all the same," the other peasant replied.

"How often?" said the old peasant. "Even if the fox swallows the poison, you can't depend on it. No one has ever been able to decide the correct dose of strychnine to kill an unknown fox!"

"So according to you," the other peasant said with a laugh, "you ought first to make his acquaintance and then ask him to dinner?"

"If it's a strong fox," said the old man, ignoring the laughter at his expense, "and it's a small dose of strychnine, at most it'll give him a slight bellyache, which won't stop him from eating your chickens."

"Obviously it's better to use plenty of strychnine," the other peasant said.

"No, it isn't," the old man replied. "If you give too strong a dose, the fox will bring it up immediately, and he'll eat your chickens with double the appetite."

"So according to you," Daniele said, "there's no defense against foxes!"

"You have to know how to go about it," the old man said, beckoning to him to approach, as if to confide a secret in his ear. "There's one infallible method," he whispered loudly enough for the others to hear. "It's to catch him by the tail with both hands and take him to the butcher's."

He burst out laughing and walked away, followed by the laughter of the others.

"What are you going to do?" Filomena asked her husband as soon as they were alone.

"I'll set the trap," said Daniele. "What do you expect me to do?"

"Today it's one thing and tomorrow it's another," the woman said with a sigh. "There's never any end to it!"

So every evening Daniele set the trap outside his chicken run and covered it with dry leaves. He also scattered about bits of meat and one or two chestnuts poisoned with strychnine. But the fox kept away.

"You've got to be patient," he would say to Silvia, who helped him in these preparations.

four

"You look rather tired," Silvia said to him.

"Do you think so?"

"You came back late again last night. That was the second time in a week. Isn't that rather overdoing it? It was nearly four o'clock!"

"I see you're a light sleeper."

"If I were your wife . . ." the girl said, without finishing the sentence.

"Would you divorce me?" asked Daniele.

"Meanwhile you've been seen by one of the neighbors, the one they call Squint-Eye."

"Yes, he squinted at me."

"His wife stopped me in the street outside the chemist's a few days ago. 'What is your father doing up and about so often in the middle of the night?' she said to me."

"I've seen her husband too. So we're quits."

"But he goes out to look after his cows."

"Everyone looks after what he can. Well, now I know how he uses his time, thanks for the information."

"I don't know if you've noticed," said Silvia, "but this year our camellias are late."

"They followed my advice," Daniele explained. "Now we shan't have to send them to the festival."

This was the time of the year when Daniele tended his orchard. It was delicate work, which he did with the care of a precision-instrument worker. His natural fondness for technique actually found a better outlet here than in the monotonous work he had used to do at the lathe. Also he had Silvia's constant companionship. Sometimes he thought the girl's smile lit up the whole farm.

To discover the parasites' nests Daniele removed the dead branches and the dead bark and moss from the trunks. When he found a hole surrounded by what looked like sawdust, he called Silvia, who put a piece of wire in the hole to kill the hidden worm.

"Isn't it cruel?" the girl asked. "Sometimes I think it's cruel!"

"There's no need to be sorry for parasites," said her father.

"Agostino calls some men parasites," Silvia remarked. "But that doesn't make it right to kill them."

"That's not the same thing," said Daniele.

"Do you think Agostino cruel?" the girl went on.

"Good gracious, no!" said Daniele. "He's a kind, warmhearted man."

"Yes, he is," said Silvia. Then she added, "He can be pitiless all the same, at any rate in words."

As soon as they had finished cleaning the tree trunks, she hurried to the house to fetch a pail of whitewash and a brush.

"Now for the powder and paint!" she said to her father with a laugh.

Every tree trunk had to be whitewashed up to a man's height. The girl had put on an old apron of her mother's for the occasion, and she covered her head with a hat made of newspaper, as painters do.

"Now they're safe," she remarked, pointing to the first whitewashed trees.

"Unless there's a hailstorm," her father pointed out. "There can always be a hailstorm."

"You mean one's never safe?" his daughter asked.

Daniele nodded. The girl grew thoughtful. Something was on her mind.

"You mean," she went on, "that no one's ever safe, even if he has done everything he ought? Even if he's honest?"

Daniele nodded again. Then he added:

"It's no use thinking about all the things that might happen."

"Why not?" Silvia went on. "Isn't that why we're whitewashing the trees?"

"But we can't protect them against hail," Daniele said. The girl's good humor vanished, and she remained thoughtful for the rest of the morning.

"If you think too much, you'll get lines on your forehead," her father remarked.

"Daddy," she asked suddenly, "do you think something dreadful might happen to Agostino?"

"Why do you ask?"

"Because I have the feeling that he seeks out misfortunes for himself. Why doesn't he just look after his own affairs like other people?"

"He's too honest," Daniele tried to explain. "He's a man and can't forget."

"You mean about his brother in prison?" Silvia asked. "Has he any news of him?"

"He's dead," Daniele said. "Didn't he tell you?"

The girl shook her head, her eyes full of tears.

"He talks easily only about things he doesn't care about deeply," Daniele explained. "That's the way he's made. It was only by chance that I found out. One evening I said to him, 'You look a bit glum, what's the matter with you?' He took a crumpled letter from his pocket and handed it to me. It was from a relative, giving him the news. I tried to say something sympathetic, but he wouldn't let me. All he said was, 'Let's talk about something else.'"

"Look, there he is!" Silvia said suddenly. "I'll leave you two alone."

"You can stay," her father said, but Silvia hurried away to hide her tears.

Agostino jumped down from a truck loaded with sacks of cement and came hurrying across the garden. He was thin, bony, agile, like an athlete.

"What's your daughter got against me?" he asked Daniele, getting his breath back.

"Nothing," said Daniele. "Her mother must have called her."

"She's becoming a strange girl, she asks me the most extraordinary questions."

"She's not a girl any longer. Perhaps that's the mistake you're making. Anyway, what's the news?"

"I'm springing my trap tonight at last," Agostino said with a wink.

"Will the fox turn up? Are you sure?"

"It made the appointment itself."

"If only my fox were so obliging," said Daniele.

"And besides," Agostino went on, "the bait is attractive."

"What bait?"

"The little dressmaker."

"You mean Nunziatina is willing? I'm surprised!"

"Of course she doesn't know everything," Agostino hastened to explain. "She only knows her own role. It's an innocent role, after all."

"Innocent? An innocent bait?" Daniele said doubtfully.

"Yes," Agostino replied. "All she has to do is to show that she doesn't know anything. That's the truth, anyway. Once she has shown good will, she'll be left in peace."

"Doesn't she find it alarming?"

"Yes, she does rather, but she knows I'll be there to protect her."

Daniele did not conceal his misgivings.

"For the first time in her life the poor woman has someone to protect her," Agostino explained. "I can't tell you how grateful she is. It's just as well that she's old."

"Will you be there only to protect her?" Daniele asked incredulously.

"As far as she knows, yes. That's all that concerns her."

"What exactly have you in mind?"

"Nothing definite," said Agostino. "The important thing is to identify the man. After that we shall see! Of course, what I should like best would be to play cat-and-mouse with him."

"Take care," Daniele said. "Don't go armed."

"I've got my head screwed on," Agostino reassured him.

Daniele did not seem entirely convinced.

"Don't you think that one of us ought to go instead of you?" he asked. "You risk expulsion."

"You're doing a great deal already," Agostino objected. "It would be absurd to risk compromising you over something trivial."

"Don't you think I ought to warn somebody from here? I mean a Ticinese," said Daniele.

"No," Agostino said. Then he added, "For an Italian fox an Italian trap."

"I should like at least to warn Franz," Daniele said. "He's a reliable fellow."

"You mean the carpenter at Minusio? I think he's ridiculous. Don't you?"

"He could keep an eye on you from a distance, and warn me or the lawyer in case of complications."

"He's not a man, he's a big baby. Do you know what they call him?"

"He's an admirable, conscientious, dependable man."

"They call him Agnus Dei! It seems that he's been in prison several times as a conscientious objector. Don't you think him ridiculous?"

"He's a brave, warmhearted man, believe me," Daniele insisted.

"And on top of it he has reconciled Karl Marx and Jesus Christ," Agostino concluded with a laugh.

The truck driver sounded his horn a few times as a hint to Agostino to hurry.

five   Until the time of the appointment Nunziatina stayed in church, kneeling in front of
the statue of Our Lady of Perpetual Succor. As it was a
weekday afternoon, the church was dark, silent, deserted,
and she was therefore able at her ease to confide all her
troubles to the holy image and to express her gratitude
for the unexpected and undeserved, and therefore truly
miraculous, aid she had received through Agostino. In
thinking of him the poor woman was unable to restrain
her tears, and this profane emotion in a sacred place
caused her to blush, for which she humbly prayed the
Blessed Virgin Mary for forgiveness. As soon as the
hour struck she left the church, greatly comforted.

It was nearly sunset. The air was golden. In the sun-
shine in the square it was barely warm, and in the side
streets it was cold and damp. Nunziatina walked quickly.
The old blue coat with velvet collar and cuffs that she

had put on for the occasion seemed rather an anticipation of the spring, but it gave an air of respectability to her small person which she felt she needed for her defense; and the black scarf draped over her gray hair, which she usually took off as soon as she came out of church, and the red-edged prayer book she carried in her left hand at the level of her heart, contributed to the same purpose.

While she walked under the arcades of the town square she was seized with a fit of giddiness, and her self-assurance was gravely shaken. Passers-by were few and in a hurry, and no one noticed the state she was in. She stopped for a moment, leaning against a café table, and then went on toward the lake. Her pale face had turned livid, and she found herself sweating from head to foot, as if she were under a hot shower. Slowly and uncertainly she walked away from the arcade and made her way toward the landing stage. Once she stopped and considered whether it might not be better to hurry back home and go to bed. At that moment Agostino passed in front of her. He did not stop, or even turn toward her, though he had certainly seen her; he had only wanted to let her see him. Nunziatina watched the strong young man walking confidently toward the lake, as he had promised. So he had not let her down. She felt relieved, and smiled, and followed him without further hesitation.

The lake was gray, with golden reflections in the curling wavelets. All the morning it had been cloudy, but now the sky had almost entirely cleared, except for some white clouds tinged with honey over the mountains above Brissago. Nunziatina made for the seat that had been indicated to her, and waited, leaning against the iron railing of the parapet. The big white boat for Stresa disappeared round the Saleggi bend. Near the landing stage gulls were chasing one another, squabbling over bits of food among the rubbish floating on the water. They rose into the air, scattered rapidly in all directions and then came back, collected into new groupings and all converged on the same spot, pecking at each other and calling hysterically, and pursuing those of their number who had managed to get hold of some more substantial morsel.

"Signorina Nunziatina, if I am not mistaken?"

This question, for which she had been waiting, was put to her by an unknown young man wearing sports clothes. To judge by his pronunciation and dark complexion, he was probably a southerner. He was rather ostentatiously carrying a Florence newspaper, as had been arranged.

"Yes," Nunziatina replied.

There was a moment's embarrassment. She should have said, Who is your favorite painter? and he should have replied, Beato Angelico, of course. Instead she said: "I presume your favorite painter is Beato Angelico."

"Of course," the young man promptly admitted. Then he added: "Shall we go to a café or somewhere? I know a very quiet patisserie."

"People would be very surprised," Nunziatina said.

"You know, I've lived here for thirty years."

"In that case let us go for a ride outside the town," the young man said. "I've got a car."

"Oh, no!" Nunziatina protested. "How could you suggest such a thing?"

They walked a little way toward Rivapiana in silence. The sun set, and it suddenly grew cooler. Nursemaids were hurrying home, pushing their prams. Only a few girls and one or two aged tourists were left by the lakeside. Nunziatina looked round nervously for Agostino; in the end she discovered him sitting on a seat, apparently absorbed in throwing bread crumbs to some sparrows that were hopping about all round him. When they passed him she looked ostentatiously in the opposite direction. A few moments later they came to a vacant seat, and she suggested to her companion that they should sit down. The young man looked all round before taking his seat beside her, and ran his two hands through his thick black hair. The gesture disclosed a medallion hanging on a chain round his wrist.

"Allow me," Nunziatina said to him, looking at the trinket. "So you are religious too!" she noted with satisfaction.

"Yes, to the point of superstition," the young man replied.

"Are you from Palermo?" she went on. "St. Rosalia is the patron saint of Palermo."

"Well, let's talk about religion another time!" the young man said with a touch of irritation.

His voice had changed; indeed he seemed a different person. The lines of his brown gaunt face hardened, and his small black lively eyes grew piercing and evil.

"What have you got to tell me?" he said.

He was sitting with his back to the town, and therefore also with his back to Agostino, so it was easy for Nunziatina not to lose sight of her protector; all she had to do was to look the young man in the face every now and then, as, indeed, good manners required.

"Yesterday," the young man said to her quietly, "you spent the whole afternoon at a lawyer's house."

"Do you know him?" asked Nunziatina. "He's an excellent person!"

"He was in Italy recently," the young man went on.

"And he came back most enthusiastic," Nunziatina assured him.

"Really?" the young man said. "He's a socialist."

"He came back most enthusiastic," the dressmaker repeated. "He's now convinced that only Italian women know how to cook rice. That is, really cook rice. His wife tried to argue with him, of course, but he wouldn't listen; he insisted that Italian rice was much better."

"And what did he talk about apart from rice?" the young man interrupted.

"He went into ecstasies about the cheese," Nunziatina went on. "Even the gorgonzola, which frankly I detest. You should have heard him!"

"I don't care a hoot," the young man said rudely. "The man's a socialist."

"He's an excellent person," the dressmaker, now sure of herself, insisted.

"Didn't he criticize us at all?" the young man said. "Didn't he tell the usual stories against us? The usual horror stories?"

Nunziatina had a moment's dismay, and pressed her prayer book to her bosom, at the level of her heart.

"Didn't he tell any lies about us?" the young man went on.

"Only about apples," Nunziatina admitted. "In the end his wife forced him to admit that our apples are not as good as Swiss or German apples. They are more floury."

"Never mind about food," the young man exclaimed, at the end of his patience. "He must have talked about other things too. He's a socialist, isn't he?"

Nunziatina wrinkled her brow and made an obvious effort to remember.

"Yes," she said. "He mentioned ties. He said that nowhere in the world do men wear such smart ties as they do in Italy."

"Almighty God!" the young man burst out.

"Oh!" exclaimed the little dressmaker, surprised and shocked at this blasphemy.

"Listen, Signorina Nunziatina," the young man said, slowly and quietly, emphasizing every syllable. "What interests me, what interests us, are political conversations. Do you know what I mean?"

"No," said Nunziatina.

The young man made a gesture of despair. Then he went on patiently:

"When you've been at the lawyer's house, or at that other gentleman's house, the surgeon's, haven't you ever heard the name of Bassanesi mentioned?"

"No," replied Nunziatina. "Who's he?"

"Haven't you ever heard the name of one Carlo Rosselli?"

"I don't think so," said Nunziatina. "Unless you mean Rosati, the gentlemen's tailor. Some say he's the best tailor in the whole canton."

"You're trying to pull my leg," the young man said angrily.

"I'm only telling you what people say," the dressmaker said. "But you're obviously at complete liberty to prefer another tailor."

The young man exploded.

"Are you going on telling me rubbish of this kind?" he said.

"How dare you talk to me like that?" exclaimed the little dressmaker.

"But, my good woman," the young man said, "don't you realize that you're wasting my time?"

"And do you suppose my time isn't valuable to me?" replied Nunziatina, cut to the quick. "Do you suppose that I've got independent means?"

"What I mean is that your information isn't of the slightest use to me," the young man explained.

"I'm not surprised," Nunziatina said. "But I've told you frankly all I know. Would you prefer me to tell you lies?"

It was impossible to doubt the little dressmaker's good faith. There was a long pause. The young man looked at his watch and decided that there was no point in going on.

"I'm afraid the whole thing has been a misunderstanding," he said.

"Perhaps you're right," said Nunziatina. "It must have been a misunderstanding."

The young man rose to his feet and looked all round, as if he were looking for someone. Nunziatina took a deep breath; she was safe. Such was her sense of relief that she felt like saying something nice to the young man before she left him.

"You're so young," she said to him kindly. "You might be my son. Why didn't you learn a trade?"

The young man looked at her furiously.

"Shut up!" he said, and went away.

All this time Agostino had not moved from his seat. Nunziatina had not let him out of her sight. When it grew darker the sparrows had left him, and there he sat, alone on the seat, with his hat pulled over his eyes, looking like an out-of-work having a snooze. But before the young man had walked ten yards Nunziatina saw Agostino spring to his feet and follow him. Did he want to talk to him? Did he want to persuade him to leave her alone? Nunziatina, with tears in her eyes, watched the two men until they vanished behind some trees.

six Daniele's misgivings about what would happen next turned out to be justified. Inevitably Agostino and the young man came to blows; violence, indeed, flared like a flash of lightning. Fortunately Franz, the carpenter, had been near, but for the rest of the evening he was unable to shake off the feeling of pain and humiliation with which the scene filled him.

"Perhaps it wasn't premeditated," Daniele tried to persuade him. "How can you be sure it was premeditated?"

"Violence and lies always go together," Franz said sadly. His strange pronunciation of Italian made him sound even more distressed.

"This isn't the time for an argument, is it?" said Daniele. "But you're not being fair to Agostino. He has always been completely loyal."

"He didn't tell me anything about his intention to attack the man," Franz replied. "I should have tried to dissuade him."

"Perhaps it wasn't premeditated," Daniele repeated.

"I'm afraid it was," said Franz. "He went for him as soon as they were alone together. It was a repulsive and degrading spectacle."

He made a grimace of disgust. Meanwhile, as it was late by now, he started putting away his tools. His was a tiny shop; there was scarcely room to move between the oak bench and the beams and boards leaning against the wall; in fact, during the day he had to stand some of his timber outside in the street beside the door.

Before he set up his shop here, as it happened, the spot had been known as the Snake Pit. Apparently it had once belonged to a wealthy priest who had stored wheat there in expectation of a shortage which would push the price up. When merchants came from the hungry town and offered him his own price for it, the place was found to be full of snakes. But that was not a story to frighten the carpenter.

Franz was fair, and as rough as the trunk of a fir tree worked with the ax. He might have been over forty, but his ruddy complexion, his physical agility and his naïveté made him seem much younger. He had settled in the Ticino some years earlier for the sake of his wife, who suffered from lung trouble, believing that the climate would be good for her. After her death he stayed on, perhaps because he had taken a liking to the people. Those who had business dealings with him liked him for his honesty; others thought him a bit cracked because of his pacifism and antimilitarism, and his familiar and confident way of talking about Christ as if He were a personal acquaintance.

That evening he was bitter and disillusioned, and this upset Daniele, who, though he did not share his utopianism, was always rather intimidated by his opinions.

"Damn it all, man, you ought to be able to understand him!" Daniele went on. "He had something personal to settle, something very recent."

"I know," said Franz. "But there's nothing worse than taking one's own private feelings into politics."

"Don't ask for too much," said Daniele. "After all, we're men, not angels!"

"But if we behave like brutes, like our enemies, how do we differ from them?" Franz replied.

Daniele made an impatient gesture.

"Do you ask me that?" he said. "Don't you know?"

Franz remained unperturbed.

"Yes, I do know," he replied. "You mean in ultimate aims. But even their ideals are perfectly good in the abstract. When you come to think of it, patriotism, order, tradition are not to be despised, are they? It's violence that makes them false and detestable."

"Well," Daniele interrupted, "this doesn't seem to me to be the occasion for this sort of discussion. When a comrade is in need, I go to his aid."

"What's that got to do with it?" said Franz, changing his tone. "If you think I want to back out, you're mistaken."

That was all that mattered to Daniele.

"Do you think it will end in court?" he asked.

"From the little that I know about these things, I should say that it will depend on the seriousness of the injuries," Franz replied.

"I suppose you can't do serious damage with your fists alone."

"You never can tell. From where I was, I saw the man go down like a log. He didn't make a sound. I ran up as fast as I could, but someone else got there first."

"Was he a local man?"

"To judge from his appearance and what he called out, I should say he was an Italian. I don't think he was there by chance. For a moment it looked as if he were going to go for Agostino, but when I came up he busied himself with the injured man. I had the impression that he called him by his name."

"He'll have been an accomplice," Daniele said.

The carpenter was standing at the entrance to his shop, looking up and down the street.

"Agostino's late," he said.

"Didn't he say he was coming here?" Daniele asked.

"He was going to have a word with the lawyer, and was coming here to meet you afterward," Franz said.

Daniele's impatience was getting the better of him.

"I'm going for a stroll," he said. "If he turns up, tell him to wait till I come back."

He walked toward the station, looking carefully all round him. Long lines of coaches were drawn up in the sidings. Two buses serving the neighboring valleys were standing in the station square. Daniele walked through the waiting room and stopped for a few moments on the platform. The only persons waiting for the train were some elderly Englishwomen, dressed like parrots in yellow and violet, and a number of porters in uniform. Because of the season and the hour, hardly anyone was about, even under the arcades of the big town square; a few foreigners, one or two pensioners and some soldiers, and that was all.

There was a little more life in the cafés, because of the regular customers who sat there for hour after hour reading the newspapers and talking. Each of these places, in accordance with cantonal tradition, had its own political color. Only tourists could go indiscriminately into any café that took their fancy; for a resident to go several times in succession to any particular one was equivalent to a profession of political faith. In such a thoroughly democratic country a change of political allegiance obviously called for no particular heroism; but it did, however, involve a change of café, *i.e.*, of an agreeable habit. Consequently it was not surprising that political changes of heart were rare.

With his friends Daniele never made any mystery of his opinions, but he had never liked café loungers, and he had a special dislike of café politicians, no matter what their party. But this evening it was important to him to find out if they had yet heard about the lakeside affray, and, if so, what they were saying about it. So he went to the café that he knew his friends went to, looked all round, and went up to the counter.

"A *grappa*," he said to the Junoesque girl with untidy hair who was serving.

As he expected, he was spotted by someone sitting

with a group round a table at the other end of the room. "Daniele!" the man called out. "Why on earth are you drinking at the counter as if you were in the land of the heathen?"

"I'm in a hurry," Daniele said. He emptied his glass at a gulp, and went over to shake hands.

"What are you discussing so conspiratorially?" he asked lightly.

They looked at each other. They were all elderly, and it was hard to place them by their appearance; they could have been pensioners. They were all shabbily dressed and ill-shaven, and were divided into smokers of cigarettes and smokers of cheap Brissago cigars, but they all looked equally tired and depressed. In front of each was an empty coffee cup, and every saucer was full of ash and cigarette ends.

"Daniele's one of us," said one of the Brissago smokers, looking round at the others. "We can tell him, can't we?"

"He's one of us, but he has never been willing to compromise himself," one of the cigarette smokers remarked. "He's never been willing to be our candidate."

"That's quite true," Daniele admitted.

"Never mind, you're one of us," several others assured him.

"Well, this is what it's about," one of them said. "In your opinion, should we or should we not insure the next Festival of the Camellias against bad weather?"

"Last year and the year before it rained," Daniele replied.

"That's the *uregiatt** argument," the cigarette smoker protested.

"It's not an argument, it's a fact," said Daniele. "My daughters came home soaked to the skin both years."

"Who's disputing that?" said several of those present. "It rained, and the municipal committee reimbursed us for the loss. That's why the *uregiatt* want the festival to be insured this year."

"And do you oppose that?" Daniele said.

"Of course!" several of those present said. "It's obvious that you live in the country. The *uregiatt* are in favor, so we've got to be against."

"Why didn't you get in first?" asked Daniele.

The embarrassment was general, but of brief duration.

"We could have got in first," one of the cigarette smokers said. "But we said to ourselves: Supposing it turns out fine this year? They'd accuse us of wasting public funds."

"I see," said Daniele. "Is that all the news?"

"What?" several men protested vigorously. "Don't you call that news?"

"Good night!" Daniele said. "They're expecting me at home."

When he left the café it was drizzling. He entered the maze of little streets behind the arcade, and sought out the house of the lawyer Zeta. The lawyer opened the door himself.

"I was expecting you," he said in unusually confi-

* Disparaging dialect word for conservatives and political priests.

dential tones. "Come in quickly; don't let the neighbors see you."

He was an elderly man, short and thickset, with a big head and chiseled features, like an actor's, and a thick gray mustache. Usually he was harassed, glum and short-tempered, but today he seemed in a strange state of animation.

"Heaven be praised for these Italians!" he exclaimed as soon as he had shut the study door behind him. "What should we do without them? We'd be bored to death."

"Where's Agostino?" Daniele asked. "I've got to talk to him."

"Without these Italians we should be bored to death," the lawyer repeated. "Sit down! Would you like a drink?"

The room was feebly lit by a table lamp with a green shade. The lawyer made Daniele sit in an old leather armchair next to a writing desk littered with law books, legal documents and letters. On the wall behind the desk were dusty portraits of Emilio Bossi and Mazzini. Shelves full of law books covered the other walls. Daniele wondered for a moment what the musty smell coming from the bookshelves might be: it was probably not mushrooms.

"I note with pleasure that you've put on weight," the lawyer said. "The healthy country life, of course."

"I don't want to flatter you, but I see that you've put on weight too," said Daniele, returning the compliment. "Where's Agostino?"

"It is our good fortune," the lawyer went on, "to live

66

on the borders of a country generously provided by nature with volcanoes. Nothing is more tedious than a hereditary democracy such as ours. Do you know that we have one of the highest suicide rates in the world?"

Daniele was not to be diverted.

"Where's Agostino?" he said.

"Have you ever wondered," the lawyer continued, "why so many old ladies from abroad spend their holidays or settle here? The explanation is that here they find themselves back in the days of their childhood. Time has stood still here since 1914; in other words, since before the Flood. That is why our country is generally spoken of as an ark of peace. Do you know what Noah's ark was?"

"Yes," said Daniele. "Two specimens of every kind of filthy animal were put in it, to preserve the species."

"Yes," said the lawyer with a broad laugh. "Two specimens of every species, a black and a red."

"You mean a gray and a pink," said Daniele. Then he asked again:

"Where's Agostino?"

The lawyer gave in.

"You're quite right to like him so much," he said with perfect seriousness. "We shouldn't waste all our affection on women. What is there so special about them, after all? Agostino, you were saying. He's a generous, warmhearted, impulsive man; he reminds me of myself when I was a youth."

"Where is he now?" said Daniele.

"Who?" the lawyer said, taken by surprise. "Myself, when I was a youth?"

"No, Agostino," Daniele repeated patiently.

"He's in a place of safety."

"I've got to talk to him."

"Impossible!"

Daniele adopted the subterfuge used in dealing with peasants at market. He rose and walked toward the door.

"I'll go and find him," he said. "I know where to look."

"Don't be silly, come back and sit down," said the lawyer. "I was waiting for you especially to ask you not to spoil my little game. The first thing the silly fellow wanted was to go and find you, but I persuaded him to keep away."

"Are the police after him?"

"Not yet. But that's all I can say."

"Do the police know about the incident?"

"They're groping in the dark," the lawyer said. "But there are certain things I shouldn't tell you. Well, just now I dropped in at the police office. My excuse was an infringement of the highway code by my son, a trifling matter. While I was there, chatting to the chief of police about one thing and another, who should drop in, of all people, but the lawyer who represents the Italian consulate. He had his excuse too, of course. D'you know him? He's that old spindleshanks with a nose like an elephant's trunk. He sniffed us all over with it, smiling all the time, trying to snuffle out what we were up to. We spent a good half hour like that, each of us studying the expression of the others, waiting for someone to give himself away. But nothing happened. But that's not the whole story. As you probably know—because otherwise my indiscretion would be unpardonable—we've got one of our people in the police force. An absolutely reliable, first-rate man. He came to see me here, downstairs, to tell me that his chief had heard a vague rumor that something serious had happened at some isolated spot this afternoon. I asked him how he found out, and he ended by coming out with it. He made me swear not to repeat what he said to a living soul. He told me that we've got one of our people in the consulate. He's not told everything, but he tries to listen, and he picks up what he can. Everyone knows what a difficult job it is. Anyway, he heard that there had been a scuffle between Italians, but he didn't know what it was about, whether it was a vendetta, or whether it was about a woman, or whether it arose out of commercial rivalry, or whether it was political, or what. He wanted to know what I thought. Do you realize that? He wanted to know what I thought, I of all people! The good man couldn't have turned up at a better moment. 'As you are one of us,' I said to him, 'as you are one of us, and a hundred per cent reliable man, I can be absolutely frank with you. The fact of the matter is that I know nothing whatever about it, nothing whatever. But, as you're one of us,' I added, 'and as you've asked me to make a suggestion, my advice is: *Cherchez la femme!*' I said to him in French. 'Italians fight only about women.' "

The lawyer winked at Daniele, and rubbed his hands with satisfaction.

"Did I do well?" he asked.

A strange, continuous noise was coming from overhead.

"Is someone playing billiards upstairs?" Daniele asked.

"No, it's mice," the lawyer explained. "For the past ten years I've been engaged in a legal squabble with the landlord about whose responsibility it is to get rid of them. Meanwhile they have been taking advantage of the situation to multiply!"

"So the injured man has not yet complained to the police?" Daniele said.

"That's not a matter for him to decide," the lawyer explained. "He's only a subordinate. Besides, an agent of that category who complains to the police burns his own tail and sets fire to his own net."

The lawyer spoke with the tone and gestures of a conjuror explaining a complicated trick.

"Just leave it to me!" he concluded with a laugh. "You can rest assured that everything will turn out all right."

"How long shall we have to wait?" Daniele asked doubtfully.

"That's absolutely impossible to say," said the lawyer. "The important thing is not to be impatient. Impatience leads to recklessness. If you can, try to visualize the strangeness of our situation. Both we and our enemies have set the whole area with traps, and we are both restricted to the same area. So we all run the risk of being hoist with our own petard. Isn't it exciting?"

The lawyer was unusually gay and animated.

"So what are we to do?" Daniele asked.

"Haven't you caught on yet?" the lawyer answered with a frown. "Nothing at all. Lie doggo."

"Impossible," said Daniele.

"I appeal to you not to spoil the game," the lawyer went on. "If that is not enough, I give you orders to that effect in the name of political discipline. We are neutral."

"I don't feel neutral," Daniele announced. "After all, I'm a man."

"I repeat that this is a matter that must be left to the lawyers. You can rest assured that, while we are talking here, our enemies are in conclave too, weighing the pros and cons of every move. They're waiting for a false move on my part, and I'm waiting for a false move on theirs."

"Didn't Agostino leave a message for me?" Daniele asked.

"No," said the lawyer.

Daniele smiled. The lawyer had made a mistake.

"In that case, there's nothing for it but to go home," said Daniele, pretending to accept the situation; and he rapidly took his departure.

It was raining in torrents. Daniele walked quickly, almost running, keeping to the sides of the houses; but he did not manage to dodge a cold douche from some defective gutters. Apart from an occasional car, the streets were deserted.

He sought out a little tavern in a side street. It was kept by a man from Bergamo, and nearly all the customers came from there too; they went to it for the sake of the Bergamo food and wine. Daniele looked through the half-open door, but it was late and the place was deserted. He was just going away again when a small, thin young woman, with a head all eyes and hair, appeared from behind the counter.

"Fancy seeing you after all this time!" she exclaimed with a laugh. "I thought you'd forgotten all about me!"

"Has Agostino been here?" Daniele asked.

"I thought you were looking for me!" said the girl, disappointed. "Won't you come in?"

"I've got something else on my mind this evening," Daniele answered, and left.

"At least let me lend you an umbrella," the girl called after him, but he had gone. At one point he had the sensation of being followed, and he tried quickening his pace. But, as his pursuer did the same, he stopped under a lamppost and let the man overtake him. He was a young Englishman who had lost his way back to his lodgings in the dark. Daniele walked with him for a bit, and showed him the way. Meanwhile he had reached Minusio. When he turned a corner near Franz's workshop he saw a shadow move in a dark doorway, and a cavernous voice called out, "Stop, I declare you under arrest!" A burst of laughter followed. It was Agostino. They crossed a yard full of building materials and went on down a steep little alley. The ground was littered with twigs and leaves brought down by the storm. A smell of rotting wood hung in the air. They reached Franz's little house. The door was half open, and a big fire was burning in the room inside.

"Franz!" Daniele called out two or three times.

He was not at home. The room was simply furnished in the style then fashionable among the working class in German Switzerland. The floor was covered with straw mats, there was a low round table in one corner, and next to it a semicircular seat fixed to the wall. A lamp with a linen shade decorated with little red squares stood on a metal shelf.

"Who's that?" asked Agostino, pointing to a photograph of an elderly, frowning, severe-looking man which was standing on the mantelpiece. Underneath it was the name Leonhard Ragaz.

"A religious socialist," Daniele explained. "A good chap. He left Church and university for the sake of the workers. But where can Franz be?"

"I think he must have gone to sleep in the carpenter's shop," Agostino said. "I know he has done so on other occasions when I've sent him refugees."

"Really?" Daniele said. "Frankly, I shouldn't be capable of it."

"I changed my mind about Franz today," Agostino said. "He's a tremendous fellow. He's got strength and agility I should never have credited him with."

"He used to play center forward for Kreuzlingen," Daniele said. "Now he's the trainer of the local team here."

"You should have seen him today!" Agostino went on. "It was just like a scene from an American film. I assure you that when I saw the second Fascist running toward me with a pistol in his hand I thought my number was up."

"You didn't have a pistol?"

"No, I took your advice, I didn't even have a penknife. But Franz intercepted him, kicked the pistol out of his hand, picked it up and flung it in the lake. It was over in a flash, much more quickly than I can tell you about it. The other man was so surprised that he stood there like a dummy. 'Look after the injured man, or you'll get what's coming to you too!' Franz said to him. Not bad for a man they call Agnus Dei!"

"I'm not surprised," Daniele said. "I never thought that his gentleness came from weakness."

"It's strange," Agostino said. "I can't understand why he stays here at Minusio. He's still a young man."

"He has his faith wherever he is," Daniele said.

"What do you mean?"

Daniele shrugged his shoulders.

Agostino went into the next room to fetch some blankets.

"We're both drenched to the skin," he said. "We may as well try to avoid pneumonia." He took off his clothes, hung them to dry on a chair near the fire and wrapped himself in a blanket. Daniele did the same. Their clothes started steaming. The two men moved their stools nearer the fire.

Wrapped in their blankets, they looked like two monks. Daniele added wood to the fire, and turned out the light to avoid rousing the curiosity of the neighbors. The raucous voice of a drunk floated in from the street. Agostino got up and started looking for something in the cupboard. He could not find it in the next room either.

"We need a drink," he remarked.

"It's no good looking for one here," Daniele said. "Franz is a teetotaler. Don't you know that he only allows teetotalers on his football team?"

"Really?" said Agostino. "If that's the case, I return to my old opinion of him," he added scornfully.

"Let's talk about you instead," Daniele suggested. "You've put yourself in a pretty pickle."

"Never mind," said Agostino.

"I thought you had more self-control."

"By the way," said Agostino, to change the subject, "don't you think our lawyer's a bit cracked?"

"Yes, he's one of us. But don't change the subject. What do you propose to do?"

"Keep out of the way for a few days. I can get a lift in a truck over the St. Gotthard."

"When would you go?"

"At about dawn, and get to Olten during the morning."

Daniele turned the clothes hanging on the chairs. Then he said:

"Would there be room for me?"

"There's always room for you."

"I could use the opportunity to clear up that little matter with the printer," he explained.

This put Agostino in a good mood.

"That'll make the trip much less boring," he said. "Now let's go to sleep. Good night." Then he added: "I was afraid I might not find you, so I telephoned your house some time ago. Silvia answered."

"Was everything all right at home? I'm worried about Silvia; she's getting more and more nervy."

"I warned her that you might not be coming home," Agostino said. "But we only talked for a moment. Silvia was worried because there was a collision between two cars somewhere near your house, and a man who was injured was carried into your yard. In your absence Filomena did not know whether it was all right to take him in."

"Anybody'd think that my wife didn't know me," said Daniele.

"That can happen if people live too close to one another for many years," said Agostino.

"Let's try to go to sleep," Daniele said. "It'll be an uncomfortable journey."

"At Bellinzona I'll buy a bottle of *grappa*," said Agostino. "It'll be freezing on the St. Gotthard in this weather. You were talking about Silvia."

"Good night," Daniele said. "Let's try to go to sleep."

seven   When Daniele got home three days later, he was immediately struck by the change of atmosphere.

"There you are at last," his wife said to him with a touch of irony.

When he went up to his room he found the staircase blocked with furniture.

"Have you had the bailiffs in?" he asked in surprise.

Luisa explained what the commotion was about. While the injured man was in the house some chairs and a divan had been moved, and now she and her sister were putting everything back in its place.

"Who was he?" Daniele asked Silvia. Instead of answering she went out onto the arcade with a rug that needed cleaning.

Luisa answered for her.

"He was an engineer or an accountant, I never really

found out," she said. "His name was Signor Cefalù. He was a very handsome young man!" she added with a touch of malice.

"How long was he here?"

"Two days. An ambulance came for him last night. The injuries weren't serious."

Daniele noticed that his younger daughter had grown taller and thinner; there was an unusually sharp look on her little goat's face. Meanwhile Silvia had come back, pulling the vacuum cleaner behind her; she was embarrassed, and did not know which way to look.

"Were we wrong to take him in?" she asked her father in a strained voice.

She looked tired and had rings under her eyes, as if she had not been sleeping.

"Have you been ill?" her father asked anxiously.

"She's only rather tired," Luisa answered for her, still laughing. "You see, Daddy, looking day and night after an injured man who wasn't so seriously injured after all, thank heaven, and you know how long the nights are at this time of year!"

"Luisa!" Silvia protested.

But Daniele had to hurry into the yard, where some Italian workmen were kicking up a row. He had engaged them to do some trench digging, and they had turned up both yesterday and the day before, only to find that he was not there.

"If we're not paid for the lost days' work we'll go to the trade union!" they were shouting. "What sort of an employer is this? Is he a farmer or a tourist?"

Daniele assured them that they would be paid their due. He took them with him, and showed them the work that had to be done.

He was going to plant a row of poplars at the end of the farm, and a row of holes to take them had to be dug at six-yard intervals. He had ordered Canadian poplars from a nursery and they would arrive as soon as the holes were dug, and there was no time to lose, as with the approach of spring the saplings would soon start sprouting, which would make transplantation risky. He spent a good part of the morning measuring and marking out the work, and for several hours forgot his other preoccupations. The workmen were soon reconciled to him. "He obviously knows what he's about," they said to one another. At about ten o'clock he gave them wine. To their great surprise, it was not watered.

When he went back to the house Daniele again noticed the strange atmosphere which had greeted him on his arrival. He had brought Silvia a shawl as a present from Agostino; it was still lying on the chair on which he had put it.

"Don't you like it?" he asked.

"It's not bad, but it's not a fashionable color," the girl answered.

"You haven't even asked how he is," her father pointed out.

"Whom do you mean?" Silvia asked in an uncertain voice.

Daniele went into the kitchen to wash. His wife was

busy cooking, and the place was filled with a good onion smell.

"Shall we stop this game of blindman's buff?" Daniele said.

"What do you mean?" said Filomena.

"I mean about the engineer or accountant, or whatever he is," Daniele said.

Filomena went and shut the kitchen door. She plucked up courage and said:

"It would be a good match."

"Oh! So it's got as far as that already, has it?" Daniele exclaimed.

"He's an accountant and lives at Varese. He's a very presentable, educated young man of good family," Filomena went on.

"So it's a case of love at first sight, is it?" Daniele said.

"He'd be just the right age for Silvia!"

"People who have to be the right age are generally conscripts."

"I've already talked to him, don't worry," Filomena assured him.

"But don't you realize that that's just what I'm worried about?"

The good woman was used to hearing her husband talk in this strain, so she went on without taking any notice:

"Before he got his present job he used to help his father. The family own a factory."

"What do they make?"

"Church candles."

Daniele wrinkled his nose.

"You ought to have known that I've never been able to stand the smell of burning candles," he said.

"They seem to have been having a slump too," Filomena went on.

"What, the churches? Thank heaven, a bit of good news at last!" exclaimed Daniele.

"No, the candlemaking business," Filomena said. "In recent years many churches have been going over to electric light."

"I see, religion reconciling itself with science!"

"So the young man looked for a job to help his family, and found one at Varese."

"And took the first opportunity of making an excursion a little way to the north and found himself a mother-in-law into the bargain."

"He's a very presentable young man," Filomena went on. "Very likeable and confidence-inspiring."

Daniele stopped her with a gesture of annoyance.

"I don't doubt it," he said. "But he's still an accountant. I can't imagine a girl like Silvia ending up as the devoted wife of a respectable little churchgoer."

"And if she likes him?" Filomena asked.

Daniele could not get over his amazement. His normally cautious, suspicious wife had changed out of all recognition. This would have made him laugh if Silvia's future had not been at stake.

"How strange life is!" said Filomena with a sigh. "Who would have believed that they would meet through a car accident?"

"But that's what they're for!" Daniele exclaimed

81

angrily. "Didn't you know? Nowadays the government thinks of everything."

"Really?" said Filomena.

The good woman found this difficult to believe.

"I'll talk to Silvia," Daniele said.

"You won't upset her, will you?" said Filomena.

The girl was hanging out clothes to dry under the arcade. Her father called her from the garden.

"Silvia!" he called out in his usual cordial tones. "Can you come and give me a hand?"

"I can't now, I'm busy," his daughter replied hesitantly.

"Later, then?" Daniele asked.

There was no reply. Daniele was left standing in open-mouthed astonishment, gazing at the arcade from which his daughter had vanished. He expected to see her reappear a moment later with her usual smile, and to hear her call out, "Just a minute, Daddy, I'm just coming." But she did not come, and he stood there as if transfixed. He walked several times round the garden, looking about him, but unable to remember what he had been intending to do only a few moments before. Everything seemed unrecognizable, and he was stunned and hurt. Fortunately, Luisa turned up that day with a bad report from school, thus providing her mother with an opportunity to talk at length at lunchtime about the unfair ways of school masters, and leaving no chance for anybody to talk about anything else. But the tension produced in the household by the stranger's brief stay became the more painful the less it was mentioned.

Silvia studiously avoided being alone with her father. When she had no excuse to be with her mother, she shut herself up in her little room on the second floor. An express letter from Varese arrived at least once a day, and answering it took a lot of time. She spent hours sitting at her desk near the window, filling sheet after sheet of bluish paper, raising her head only to look at every car that passed along the main road on its way to or from the frontier. As soon as a letter was finished she got on her bicycle and took it to the post office; and she never lost an opportunity of being away from home.

One afternoon she went to Bellinzona to see an aunt, who telephoned Filomena to say that the girl would be staying for dinner. If this was an excuse to allow the family to talk about the accountant without Silvia's embarrassing presence, it was certainly not her mother's idea; for she had long since given up hope of influencing her husband by anything she said. But that evening Daniele was in an unusually expansive mood, and actually praised the ham omelet. "It's just right," he said. Filomena finished the soup left over from lunchtime, and repeated for the nth time that she always thought soup better when it was reheated. She had an old shawl over her shoulders, and ate with bent head, chewing slowly, with a regular, revolving motion of the jaws, like a cow. Luisa sat beside her, drinking her tea and stroking the tail of a white kitten she held in her arms.

"I can't remember how many years you've had that shawl," Daniele said to his wife. "Didn't you have it before we were married?"

"It's a bit faded," Filomena admitted, "but it's still soft. Perhaps I'll have it dyed."

"Don't think of having it dyed and giving it to me," said Luisa. "I've already got a dress cut out of an old coat that belonged to Grandma!"

"And what's wrong with that?" said Filomena. "Once upon a time even good families used to have woolen and silk clothes that lasted for generations."

She knew that this was a theme on which she did not risk her husband's displeasure. Indeed, he intervened on her side.

"In my time," he said, turning to Luisa, "when you wanted to praise a piece of material, you didn't say it was pretty, you said it was strong."

Filomena did not allow the favorable moment to pass.

"As Silvia's out," she said, "perhaps we might have another talk about that young man."

"As you wish," Daniele replied.

"I think he's an honest man," she went on.

"Honest?" he said. "You know what I mean by an honest man?"

"Certainly," she replied, but with hesitation in her voice. "An honest man's an honest man. Wasn't my father an honest man, for instance? And my uncles were always regarded as honest men too, and everyone respected them."

"I see you haven't the slightest inkling of what I mean by an honest man," Daniele announced. Then he added, "I mean, honest in relation to the times we live in."

This left Filomena openmouthed.

"Couldn't we discuss this in rather simpler terms?" she suggested timidly.

Daniele did not answer, but went on staring impassively into the fire.

"As you know, I'm not used to getting my way with you, and perhaps I don't even want to," she went on after a few moments. "But I want at least to talk to you."

She signed to Luisa, who rose and went out of the room, taking the kitten with her.

"Did you think you knew Silvia?" Filomena went on. "Did you think she was like you?"

Evening had fallen. The lower part of the garden that could be seen through the kitchen window was rapidly disappearing in the dark. The tops of the trees were tinged with blue, like *aubergines*, and the silhouette of the mountains turned wine-red. Daniele threw some logs on the fire.

"What do you think of what I've been saying?" his wife asked him.

"What have you been saying?" he replied.

"Haven't you been listening?"

"No."

"I was talking about Silvia."

"I'll try and talk to the girl," Daniele said.

One day when she came home she found her father sitting under the arcade, repairing a sulphur spray.

"I've got to go to Val Verzasca," he said to her with a smile. "Would you like to come with me?"

"All right," Silvia answered after a moment's hesitation. She knew that this was only an excuse, but in the end she would have to have things out with her father.

They took the post-bus to Aquino. Daniele took with him a bag of seed peas for a friend there. The only other passengers were some old peasant women with empty baskets, and some secondary-school boys. Silvia kept her eyes glued to the landscape, though she knew it like the back of her hand, and it had nothing to offer her. The lake was like a big gray sheet with long black streaks in it, surrounded by greeny-brown blobs of willows, alders and poplars. Signs of spring had multiplied; in particular, there hung in the air the delicate odor of earth that had been turned to take the March sowings, as well as of dry, recently burnt brushwood, of the first sticky buds and perhaps also of the seeds recently sown in the furrows. On the way up the valley there were a few flurries of rain, though the sun continued to shine. It was a poor valley. The rocks on the mountainside looked like worn-out, decayed bones.

"In the old days people used to say that this was the kind of weather the fox got married in," Daniele said to his daughter, with a smile.

"Why?" she asked.

"Perhaps because the fox is a mean animal," Daniele tried to explain. "To save expense it chooses treacherous weather like this for its wedding, when no one expects it."

Silvia remembered this when she got out of the bus at the top of the valley and saw a magnificent rainbow.

"Look!" she said. "There's heaven rejoicing with the fox!"

"Yes, heaven's on the side of the crafty," her father admitted.

Aquino is an agglomeration of small, dark houses. Today it seemed uninhabited. The friend for whom Daniele had brought the peas lived in a tumbledown little house in an alley near the church. A goat was tied to a ring in the wall, and the whole alley was filled with an acute stable smell.

"Antonio!" Daniele called.

The door was difficult to open, but eventually it yielded, and a little old woman appeared, dressed in black; she was so small that she looked as if she had shrunk.

"Maria Rosaria, how are you?" Daniele said. "Isn't your son in?"

"Antonio's in the fields," the old woman replied. "But who are you?"

The old woman recognized him before he had time to answer.

"Daniele! Oh, what a delightful surprise!" she exclaimed. "And who is this lovely creature? Your daughter? As grown-up as this already? Come in. I'll send for Antonio immediately."

"Thank you, but don't put yourself out," said Daniele. "We didn't come for a visit; we're just on an outing. I've brought a few peas for Antonio to sow."

"Are you sure you won't come in?" said the old woman, disappointed. "Antonio'll never forgive me!"

But Daniele was not to be persuaded.

"Another time," he repeated to the old woman several

times. "Today I'm walking back with my daughter. We both want to be together for a bit."

They set off home without further delay.

"What will your friend Antonio think?" Silvia said reproachfully as soon as they were out of the village.

"About what?" Daniele asked.

"About you, about us. Why didn't we wait?"

"He won't see anything strange in a father and daughter wanting to go for a walk."

Silvia looked all round; this part of the valley was rather monotonous and grim.

"It doesn't seem to me a place worth going such a long way to just for the sake of the walk," she remarked.

This was not a promising beginning. They went on a little way in silence. Daniele surreptitiously looked at his daughter, and could not get over his embarrassment and surprise. In the past he had always held her hand, and Silvia had liked him to. Now it was out of the question. The girl was in a bad mood.

"Must we go back the same way?" she asked.

"There's no other."

"Isn't there a path along the stream at the bottom of the valley?"

"I don't think so," Daniele said, but as he was inclined to give in to all his daughter's whims, he added, "We can try if you like; we're not in a hurry."

They found a steep path which wound its way down to the stream between clumps of brier and juniper. The stream here leaped over a rock several feet high, and underneath it was a pool of water so clear that you could make out every pebble at the bottom.

"What a strange-looking cake!" exclaimed Silvia, pointing to a streak of sandy substance lying under the water.

"That's trout's eggs," her father explained.

"Don't they get scattered by the stream?"

"In autumn the trout make their way upstream," her father explained. "The females seek out well-protected, rocky places to lay their eggs in. When they've found a suitable spot, they move away the pebbles with their tails and lay their eggs, which stick to the rock."

"Is that how trout are born?"

"That's not the whole story," Daniele went on. "The eggs have to be fertilized by the males. They follow in the females' tracks and squirt their own milky liquid on the rocks where the eggs are. A few days later the eggs start opening."

Silvia was sitting at the edge of the water, marveling at the miracle of the yellowish deposit waiting for fertilization.

"At this moment I feel envious of the trout," she murmured.

"I can well believe it," Daniele said. "You're worried about what your father thinks."

Silvia did not deny it.

"Shall we talk about it?" Daniele said. "The times when parents arranged their children's marriages are over, but I can't help having views on the matter. As I'm fond of you, I'm worried about your future."

"I'm terribly sad that you don't share in my happiness," Silvia said.

The girl's eyes had filled with tears. For a moment

contact between father and daughter seemed to have been re-established.

"Do you feel really happy?" her father asked.

"Yes, tremendously," Silvia replied. "I didn't know one could be so happy. Now at last I know what love is."

"What you felt previously was not love?"

"No, I realize that now. It was liking, esteem, sympathy, anything you like, but not love," Silvia said.

"I was hoping for an unordinary man for you, that's all."

"A hero?"

Daniele ignored the irony.

"No, simply an honest man."

"I don't think the man I've chosen is dishonest."

"He's allowed to go freely backward and forward across that damned frontier with a regular passport. That's enough to give me a pretty clear idea of him."

"He's not interested in politics."

"Under a dictatorship that's one of the most comfortable ways of being dishonest."

Silvia shrugged her shoulders.

"I'm trying hard to understand you," her father went on. "I suspect it's a temporary infatuation. I suspect he's a handsome young man."

"I've met other handsome young men," Silvia replied. "Besides, when he was brought into the house his face was covered with bandages. It was his voice that first attracted me. It was a frightened, imploring, gentle voice. He talked to me about his childhood all night. Next morning I felt that I had always known him, and I had the feeling that each of us needed the other."

The girl paused for a moment, and then said, with an obvious effort:

"I'm sorry about Agostino."

"You're under a moral obligation to let him know, if you haven't yet done so," her father remarked.

"Will he be staying at Aarau for long?" Silvia asked, betraying a secret wish.

"I don't think so," Daniele answered. "He's only got to finish the job he's doing there for his firm."

"Doesn't it depend on you how long he stays?" asked Silvia.

"Not in the least," her father replied, annoyed at the question. "What on earth makes you think that?"

The abruptness of his reply restored the previous coolness and distance between them. The outing had failed in its purpose. Silvia's face looked as if it had turned to stone.

They walked on along the path at the bottom of the valley, but did not get far, because soon the path crossed the stream and started zigzagging steeply up the opposite slope. So they had to turn back and clamber up the hill to the main road. When they got there Silvia was perspiring and out of breath. Luckily an empty truck stopped, and they gladly accepted the lift which the driver offered them. They knew this man, who worked for the same firm as Agostino, and Agostino soon cropped up in the conversation.

"I hope he comes back soon," said the driver. "He

and I have rows every now and then, but I can't help liking him."

"You can't help liking him if you know him," Daniele said.

"He's a man made for friendship," the driver went on. "He's made for friendship, just as others are party men, or church men, or businessmen."

"There's nothing like friendship," Daniele said.

They went on talking about friendship for quite a time, until Silvia began yawning ostentatiously.

"I beg your pardon," she said. "I know it's not very friendly."

eight   A few days later news spread round the cafés in the little town that the police were about to reveal the full details of a political brawl that had recently taken place, and that the result would be a public scandal from which both sides would suffer. On the same day, though entirely without collusion, both the lawyer Zeta and the leader of the other party referred in the course of café conversation with their political friends to an obscure plot to wreck the forthcoming Festival of the Camellias. This would have a serious effect on the influx of foreign tourists. According to Zeta, the plot had been hatched by the *uregiatt* in collusion with foreigners; his right-wing counterpart more prudently confined himself to denouncing intrigue by the usual enemies of local traditional custom. The objective of both sides, however, was the same: it was to intimidate the police.

Alarm spread like lightning from the café conventicles down the arcades of the principal square and into the neighboring maze of streets. The festival was in danger, the good name of the neighborhood was gravely threatened, the old ladies from abroad would leave. The little town awoke from its sleep with a start and panicked. Radicals, socialists, and *uregiatt* ended by forgetting their differences and uniting in the face of the common peril. A long-haired journalist, a furious smoker of Brissago cigars, coined the slogan that the gravity of the situation called for. This was: Politics divides us, but the festival unites us. The local chief of police was thus given time to consult his superiors. In fact, toward evening when the festival committee approached him for assurances, he was in a position to set their fears at rest. To save the reputation of his force, he ended by trying to demonstrate that he was not yielding to any kind of pressure.

"A brawl?" he exclaimed, as if he had just landed from the moon. "What brawl are you referring to, gentlemen? There has been no inquiry here into any brawl."

Nunziatina knew nothing of all these maneuvers. She never read the papers, did not frequent the cafés and had no friends who frequented them. She did not even know that there had been any violent sequel to her conversation with the young man from Palermo, the devotee of St. Rosalia. She had nearly forgotten the dreadful anxiety from which she had suffered that afternoon, and all that remained in her memory was a feeling of great gratitude to Agostino. Indeed, as an earnest of it she would have liked to offer him her humble services—unpaid of course. Why should he not bring her his washing once or twice a month, or let her do his mending? She would have felt it a pleasure to do these things for him. But she had not seen him again, and this behavior of his, first warm-hearted and generous, and then discreet, confirmed the nobility of his character in her eyes. Thus the little dressmaker's life had returned to its gray, monotonous groove. Indeed, her principal worry at this time was her eyesight; it was growing weaker, and she was finding it harder and harder to thread a needle.

When she received a summons to present herself at the police station, she went there promptly and without a trace of anxiety. Indeed, to avoid having to go there twice, she took with her her tax, electric light and milk receipts.

"You see?" she said to the policeman. "Everything's in perfect order."

She was therefore taken utterly aback when the man read out to her an order of expulsion. At first she could not believe her ears, and the man had to repeat it several times. She could not believe that such a Draconian measure could possibly apply to her. But in the end the short thickset man sitting behind the desk succeeded, in the brusque manner peculiar to his calling, in convincing her that it was true.

"But how can it be possible?" she said incredulously, gazing round her in bewilderment.

The room was clean and tidy, with a vague smell of disinfectant, like a hospital waiting room. No hygienic measures, however, could affect the mysterious capacity it shared with all police stations all over the world of striking terror into the hearts of the most innocent individuals summoned to it. Poor Nunziatina soon felt the influence of this, though without knowing why.

"But how can it be possible?" she implored the policeman.

"How do I know?" he answered. "My duty is to carry out orders."

"What crime have I committed?"

"None," the policeman assured her. "If you were charged with any crime, you would have to appear in court."

"Then why are you sending me away?" she asked, bursting into tears.

This upset the guardian of law and order.

"The police are under no obligation to give explanations," he replied harshly.

"I know, I know," Nunziatina said between her sobs. "But it's the ruin of me!"

The policeman shrugged his shoulders.

"There's nothing I can do about it," he repeated.

"I've worked all my life," the poor woman started lamenting. "I've worked all my life. I've never given offense to anyone, and I've never had anything to do with politics."

For a moment the policeman was touched with compassion. This was sufficient to restore his natural, rather sheeplike, expression.

"Perhaps that's the mistake you made," he said. "If

you were in politics, perhaps you'd have protection."

He promptly regretted having let slip this remark. The severity of police discipline had not eliminated from his mind all trace of the hesitancy he had felt in his youth when he had been torn between becoming an elementary-school master, which his mother had wanted him to be, and an innkeeper, which his father had favored. In the end it had been his excellent marksmanship that had caused him to make up his mind to become a guardian of the law.

However, the implications of his incautious remark altogether eluded poor Nunziatina, who was a complete stranger to the sad realities of life. Sitting there crumpled on the bench against the wall, she looked older, weaker, more pathetic than ever. Even her tears were pathetic. For a time the policeman pretended to ignore her, and started consulting the papers on his desk. When her sobs subsided a little, she started again.

"Can a person be ruined without even being given an explanation?" she burst out. "Without being given a chance to defend himself, to prove his innocence, to show that the whole thing is a mistake?"

"Of course he can," the policeman replied with vigor. "Not if he's a citizen of the country, but if he's a foreigner, of course he can. Ask any lawyer you like, and he'll confirm what I say."

He picked up a piece of paper and went on:

"In your case the reason stated is just the single word 'undesirable.' That satisfies the requirements of the law. Now you may go."

The strange word "undesirable" stopped Nunziatina's flood of tears. She thought she saw a ray of hope.

"What does it mean?" she asked curiously.

"Have you forgotten Italian?" the policeman asked with a touch of irony. "Well, it simply means that you are no longer wanted in our country."

"Then it must be a mistake," Nunziatina exclaimed. "A case of mistaken identity! Heaven help me, but I've never been wanted in my life, even when I was a girl! Excuse me, but how can they say now that I'm no longer wanted? I don't want to be wanted; all I want is to be allowed to go on working in peace."

The policeman frowned severely at her. The law has no room for play with words.

"Will you leave this room of your own accord," he asked, "or shall I have to eject you?"

Nunziatina's tiny ray of hope was snuffed out like a candle.

"Where am I to go?" she asked.

"Wherever you like."

"I've lived here for thirty years."

"And you dare to complain!" the policeman exclaimed with genuine indignation. "You've lived for thirty years in a country which isn't yours, and you dare to complain?" he said.

"All I meant is that I don't know where to go," Nunziatina murmured.

"The world is large," the policeman said with an expansive gesture, "and you're not a girl any more."

"If only I were!" Nunziatina exclaimed, bursting

into tears again. "How can I start all over again at my time of life?"

"Now you've really taken up enough of my time," the policeman said. "For the last time I must ask you to leave!"

Nunziatina rose with difficulty and made for the door, but then she turned and asked another question.

"What am I to do with my furniture?" she said.

"Whatever you like," the policeman answered. "You can send it wherever you like."

"But where?"

"Anywhere you like. Florence, Paris, Lisbon, or Java."

"It's not worth the cost of transport."

"Sell it, then."

"Those old sticks? Nobody would buy them! They're stained, rickety and falling to pieces."

"Well, that's not a matter that concerns us," said the policeman, at the end of his patience.

"Then I'll put them out in the street," Nunziatina said with a shrug of the shoulders, again making toward the door. The policeman dashed after her as if he had been bitten by a dog.

"Wait a moment!" he exclaimed. "Wait a moment! You're not speaking seriously, are you? You're not really thinking of causing a scandal in the public street? Don't you realize the disturbance it would cause? And on the eve of the festival?"

His voice and behavior were human for the first time. He appealed to Nunziatina's sense of human decency, as one human being to another.

"Come, come, be reasonable," he said, with a smile. "You wouldn't do that on the eve of the festival, would you?"

His appeal was not in vain. Nunziatina repented of her thoughtlessness in having uttered what might seem like a deliberate threat.

"No, I shan't, don't alarm yourself," she said, and left.

Still stunned by the blow, she started walking quickly and aimlessly up and down under the arcades, like a mouse in a trap; and finally she took refuge in church. Once more fate had suddenly deposited her on the edge of an abyss, and in the most senseless and incomprehensible, indeed obviously absurd and ridiculous, manner. To Nunziatina the police decision was so fantastic that she did not even try to find an explanation for it. It was another brick that had fallen on her poor head, another misfortune, like her previous misfortunes. While she knelt humbly before the row of burning candles at the feet of Our Lady of Perpetual Succor, she remembered the anguish she had suffered before meeting the young man from Palermo. That time, however, everything had turned out all right, just as Agostino had foreseen. Thanks to his advice and aid and presence. How was she to find the good man now? While she prayed she also remembered Daniele, an abrupt man, but with a good heart all the same. Perhaps he might be able to help her to find her protector.

Hurriedly she finished her prayers and went to a telephone box. To avoid appearing ridiculous (the word "undesirable" was still buzzing in her ears), as soon as she got through she tried to explain to Daniele in veiled terms why she so urgently needed to find Agostino again. But there were some things that Daniele did not like discussing on the telephone, and the result was a somewhat confused and confusing conversation.

"Do you understand what I'm saying?" Nunziatina asked after every sentence.

"No, I haven't the slightest idea what you're talking about," Daniele answered.

She started all over again, but Daniele interrupted, and said it wasn't any good, he couldn't make out what she was driving at. In the end he suggested that she should come and see him straightaway.

nine

Daniele's old house reflected the warm, golden light. The rose tree that climbed the wall to the height of the arcade had put out hundreds of tiny reddish leaves. The sunlight caressed the tops of the trees in the orchard with the gentleness of a dove.

"Wait till you see how magnificent it is at the end of April," Silvia said with pride to Signor Cefalù.

"I shall certainly make a point of not missing it," he replied with a smile.

Some primulas had come out at the foot of the low, dry wall that ran down one side of the garden, and Silvia had picked some for her guest.

Her father was working in the garden, and she had appealed to him to put in an appearance and not be late.

"I'm not presentable," Daniele had objected. "I've only just finished the manure heap!"

"You can wash," his daughter had answered. "If you

103

hurry, you can even have a bath! You can't refuse to see him, as he has come specially all the way from Varese."

"He didn't come for my sake," said Daniele.

"But he did," Silvia replied. "Isn't it natural that he should want to meet my father?"

In the end Daniele agreed to put in an appearance.

"Don't be late," the girl had insisted. "He's got to go back this evening; he has only a few hours."

Silvia looked prettier, fresher, more animated than ever. She wore a new pink-and-white dress which suited her admirably, and in her chestnut hair she had put a magnificent red camellia which a girl friend had sent her from Ascona. Daniele stood looking admiringly at her as she hurried back to the house, and smiled.

From behind the laurel bushes where he was standing Daniele caught a glimpse of the young man on his arrival. He was of average height, athletic-looking, slim, smartly dressed and with a thin, dark face; in short, his appearance was by no means unattractive. Daniele seemed resigned. He had decided that if his daughter, who was no fool, had fallen so passionately in love with this Signor Cefalù, she must have discovered some out-of-the-ordinary quality in him. Signor Cefalù had brought her a present, a volume of reproductions of the principal works of Bernardino Luini.

Silvia thanked him, and she and her mother started looking at the illustrations together. But after the first few pages Silvia said with a smile:

"Oh, but I think we've got it already!"

"Never mind, I'll change it," the young man said, smiling too.

"I'll go and make sure," said Silvia, making for the stairs.

The young man hesitated, and then followed her without being explicitly invited.

"Let me see your books," he said. "I don't want to give you anything you have already."

Filomena watched the young couple dashing upstairs, and sighed. Perhaps she thought they were seizing the opportunity to be alone together for a few moments. The young man caught up with Silvia at the top of the stairs, just outside the door of the little room known in the family by the impressive name of "study."

"When a race ends in a draw, there ought to be a prize for both winners," the young man announced.

They spent the next few moments in a close embrace. The door of the little room was locked.

"Daddy's very jealous of his papers," Silvia explained with a laugh.

"And of his elder daughter?" said the young man.

"I'm afraid so," she replied.

The girl tried the door with her key, but it would not open.

"I've had a very touching letter from my father," Signor Cefalù said. "With your permission, I propose to read it later, in your father's presence. That will give him a better idea of the spirit of our family."

"Are they well at home?" Silvia asked, believing it to be her duty.

"Very well, thank you. My father says, among other things, that he lit a big candle in church to invoke the blessings of heaven upon us."

"A candle?"

"Yes, a big candle."

"Do you mean," Silvia said in embarrassment, "that in your part of the world even grown-up men do that sort of thing?"

Signor Cefalù thought that he must have expressed himself badly.

"I was talking about a sacred candle," he explained. "Aren't they used here?"

"We use electric light," said the girl.

Fortunately the conversation was interrupted at this point by the yielding of the door which she had been trying to open. Inside the little room culture was represented by a shelf consisting principally of school and New Year gift books. There was also a row of German books from the Zürich Book Guild.

"You know what a book guild is?" Silvia asked. "You don't? My father will explain it to you."

"There's Luini," she added a moment later, taking a volume from the shelf.

"And were all those your school books?" the young man asked with a smile.

"Yes," she answered. "Tedious textbooks, ghastly grammars, vile vocabularies."

Papers piled on the desk and chairs were probably connected with the management of the farm. The young man looked round with greater and greater curiosity.

In one corner there was a pile of political pamphlets in packets.

"Strange," he muttered.

"What's strange?" asked the girl.

The young man was unable to conceal his sudden embarrassment.

"Strange dictionaries," he remarked.

"They're the dictionaries used in our schools," said Silvia.

"Strange schools, strange teachers!"

"Yes, our mathematics master was a bit crazy," the girl said, in order not to contradict him.

The young man wiped his brow, which was covered with sweat.

"Don't you find it very hot?" he said.

At that moment her mother called out from downstairs:

"Silvia, won't you come and make the coffee?"

"We'll be down in a moment," Silvia answered through the doorway.

The young man seemed not to hear; he was staring at the books, in a daze.

"Shall we go down?" Silvia said with a smile. "Don't let's make the family suspicious!"

"Can I stay here for a moment or two?" the young man stammered. "Your school books fascinate me."

Later Silvia decided that the young man was already in a state of extreme agitation when he said this, but at the time she attributed his change of voice to the fascination he mentioned. So she left him alone in the little room on the second floor, perhaps for five minutes, perhaps for ten.

Meanwhile, Luisa had come back from school, and the three women, gay and excited, got busy in the kitchen.

"You lay the table while Silvia makes the coffee," Filomena said to her younger daughter. "Meanwhile, I'll look after the apple tart."

At Silvia's insistence even old Filomena had put on her best clothes and had taken from the jewel box a necklace reserved for great occasions.

"You'd better watch out, Silvia," Luisa said to her elder sister. "You realize that these are your finals! Italian young men, you know, judge girls first by their ankles, and then by the way they make coffee."

Silvia involuntarily glanced down at her ankles.

"Thank God, you've got nothing to fear," her mother said with a smile.

Luisa was just arranging the embroidered mats on the table when hurried footsteps were heard coming down the stairs.

A moment later the young man appeared in the doorway. His appearance took the three women aback. He was panic-stricken, ashen, distraught.

"What's the matter?" Silvia just had time to ask.

"Excuse me!" he muttered. "Excuse me! Excuse me! . . . I've got to go! I can't stay!"

Then he turned and ran as if the devil were at his heels. Soon afterward there was the sound of his car being started up and driven away.

The three women stood dumfounded, rooted to the spot, looking at one another as if they could not believe their eyes.

"What can be the matter with him?" exclaimed Filomena. "Has he gone out of his mind?"

For a short time this seemed to be the only possible explanation. In his hurry the young man had even left his camera on a chair by the front door.

"I don't know, I don't understand," said Silvia, stunned by the rapidity of the scene. "He seemed all right, only a bit nervous, perhaps."

She was seized by a convulsive fit of sobbing. Luisa went over and tried to comfort her.

"I'll go and see!" said Filomena.

She went up to the second floor. The study door was wide open. Inside there was chaos. The floor was strewn with papers, the drawers of the desk had been pulled out and overturned, packets of pamphlets had been untied. When their mother came downstairs with slow and halting footsteps and reappeared in the kitchen, her daughters realized that something grave had occurred.

"It was very unwise to let him into the study," she said in an anguished voice. "He found your father's papers. He rummaged in the drawers. He may have taken away addresses. Oh, God, oh, God! What shall we do now? How shall we tell Daniele?"

As soon as her mother's words suggested to Silvia a possible explanation of the young man's behavior which had not occurred to her, her tears ceased, and she looked incredulously at her mother. She exclaimed several times: "What do you say? What do you say? It's impossible. Impossible!" Then she fell into a stunned silence.

"Take her to her room and stay with her," her mother said to Luisa.

Crushed and overwhelmed, the poor woman went to the kitchen window to see whether her husband was coming. His delay showed that he was unaware of the young man's flight. Should she, or should she not, go and tell him? At last she saw him in his shirt sleeves, washing at the fountain.

There was good reason for his delay. Not long before he had seen Nunziatina coming up the garden path, and he had gone to meet her; he had wanted to avoid talking about Agostino in the presence of his family and their guest. The little dressmaker seemed very agitated.

"Do you know the young man who just ran out of the farm gate?" she asked, hardly able to get the words out in her excitement.

"I don't know whom you're talking about," Daniele had answered.

Nunziatina went up to him and, though no one would have been able to hear her even if she had spoken normally, whispered into his ear something that greatly astonished him.

"Are you sure?" he had asked.

"I think so," the terrified little dressmaker replied.

"That's a grave thing to say," Daniele had replied. "It's not a thing to say lightly."

"I'm not speaking lightly," said the dressmaker.

"Wait till I come back," he said.

He washed quickly, and hurried to the house.

"Where is he?" he asked his wife at the kitchen door.

"He's gone," she managed to stammer out.

"What? Already?" exclaimed Daniele.

"Yes, he's gone," Filomena murmured, taking the necklace from her neck.

"Didn't you want to introduce me?" Daniele said angrily. "Didn't he come to meet me?"

"He's gone!" Filomena repeated. "Or rather, he ran away. Daniele, I don't know how to tell you. A great misfortune has happened."

"So Nunziatina was right!" Daniele exclaimed.

"Nunziatina?"

"Just now, outside our house, she thought she recognized a man who's in the Fascist secret police."

"It's been a great misfortune," Filomena agreed.

"But why did he run away?" Daniele asked. "Did he suddenly think he was going to be recognized?"

"No," Filomena said. "We didn't suspect him, and he didn't suspect us. We never mentioned politics. But just now, by pure chance, he went to your study and discovered your papers. . . ."

Daniele did not wait for more. He dashed to the top of the house three stairs at a time. Filomena expected to hear loud curses and the smashing of furniture. Perhaps that was what she wanted to hear; perhaps she felt that it would clear the air. Instead, there was dead silence. The time she spent waiting at the foot of the stairs seemed an eternity. When Daniele reappeared, grim and silent, she was terror-stricken. She went toward him with clasped hands and repeated:

"It's been a great misfortune. Our poor, poor Silvia!"

He put his finger to his lips to bid her be silent.

"One piece of advice," he said quietly. "Let her keep out of my way! Don't let me set eyes on her. I might be capable of killing her!"

He went to the corner where the telephone was and locked himself in. He sat for a few moments beside the telephone, thinking. His face looked like the face of a blind man, like a mask. Nevertheless he managed to speak with apparent calm.

"Hullo," he said. "Is that you, Antonio? Pay careful attention to what I am going to say. Mother has fallen ill. Yes, gravely ill. Tell the people you know about. Good luck."

He stayed by the telephone, and hesitated for a moment. Then he dialed another number.

"Hullo? Is that Ponte Tresa? I want to talk to the electrician, please. Hullo. Gaspare, is that you? Mother has been taken ill. Yes, a short time ago. I'll call you again tomorrow, but not from home."

He put down the receiver, went upstairs and came down again with two boxes full of papers.

"Bring me a lot of wood and a bottle of petrol," he ordered Filomena. "Help me to light a big fire as quickly as possible and then leave me alone."

The auto-da-fé lasted for half an hour.

When Filomena went out into the garden to feed the pigeons, she found Nunziatina squatting on a stool at the bottom of the path, half asleep. She looked like a little schoolgirl being punished.

"What are you doing here?" Filomena asked.

"Your husband told me to wait," the little dressmaker said apologetically.

"He won't be able to come now, he's busy," Filomena said. "You must excuse him; he'll see you another time."

"What has happened?" Nunziatina asked timidly.

"Nothing," Filomena replied. "Nothing at all. What could happen?"

That night Daniele got home very late. He flung himself on his bed without undressing, and he was up again at dawn. When he left the house, he did not reply to his wife's greeting, or tell her where he was going, or whether he would be back for lunch or dinner. They waited for him in vain. Silvia spent the whole morning lying on her bed in her room, and Luisa stayed with her, doing her homework or sewing. The house was as desolate as if someone had died. The few words that were said were spoken in a whisper. The farm was buried in thick mist, and only the tops of the trees were visible. It was so dark that the light had to be kept on in the downstairs rooms. When Filomena went up to tell her daughters that lunch was ready, Luisa said that they did not want any.

Filomena had no lunch either. The rest of the endless afternoon passed in oppressive silence. There were two brief telephone calls. Luisa answered and took two rather cryptic messages for her father. These upset the girl more than ever.

"How is Silvia? What does she say?" her mother asked.

"She doesn't say anything," the girl replied. "She looks at me, but doesn't answer when I speak to her."

"Does she cry, at least?"

"No."

"If only she'd cry!" her mother exclaimed.

"What's the good of crying?" the girl asked.

"If a misfortune happens, the only thing to do is to cry," said her mother.

"Wouldn't it be better to try and do something?"

"What?"

"Anything."

"If it's a real misfortune, there's nothing to do but cry."

"When is Daddy coming back?" the girl asked.

"My dear girl, I haven't the slightest idea. He didn't say."

"Where is he? I might go and find him."

"I don't know. I assure you I haven't the slightest idea where he is."

She stopped answering the girl's questions, which were those by which she was tormented herself, and the girl went and sat in the corner of the hearth and began sobbing quietly. But toward evening, when someone suddenly knocked loudly at the door (it was a rather deaf neighbor who had come to tell them to be sure to set the trap that night because the fox had been seen in the

114

neighborhood again), it was too much for the girl's taut nerves; a fit of wild panic seized her, followed by convulsive weeping and moaning. It was difficult to calm her. Her mother had to take her on her lap and soothe her as if she were a little girl again. As soon as she could speak, the girl again started asking questions.

"Why has Daddy left us?"

"He hasn't left us," her mother answered. "You can rest assured that he'll never, never leave us; he loves us too much."

"Then why does he do these things?" said the girl. "If he loves us, why does he do these dangerous, secret things?"

"That's something I can't explain to you," the poor woman sighed.

"Aren't you his wife?"

"All I can say is that he has always been like that; he was like that even before we were married. I can't tell you the worry and anxiety it has caused me. I hoped that with time and a growing family he'd give it up, but . . ."

"But why does he do it? What does he get out of it?"

"Nothing. Nothing whatever. On the contrary, it costs him money and endless trouble. But he puts into it all his pride and honor."

"What?"

"His pride and his honor as a man. I'm afraid that life would have no meaning for him without it."

Filomena's lips trembled as she spoke. Luisa felt sorry for her and did not go on. Her mother started weeping again without restraint. It was her way of accepting life and her condition as a woman. She had lived all her life under the shadow of disaster; she had expected it for many years; she seemed to have been born expecting it and at last it had come. Its full shape had not yet been revealed, but unquestionably it had come.

ten   Daniele soon spotted Agostino waiting for him in the crowd of travelers and porters at Aarau station, and he followed him at a distance. Still at a distance, but without losing sight of each other, they spent some time strolling through solitary streets and alleys, stopping at a shop window occasionally to see if they were being followed. Finally Agostino waited for him at a corner, and they went on together. Daniele told him what had happened, starting with the phony car crash and not omitting what he knew about Silvia and the young man. Agostino kept interrupting his friend's story with great oaths but, when Silvia was mentioned, he fell silent; what her father told him took his breath away. For him too all this was a double blow.

They went on walking quickly and aimlessly for some time. They looked like two men just escaped from prison, or father and son who had run away from home. Daniele had the sturdiness and lumbering gait of a cart horse; Agostino looked like a fanatic desperately looking for someone to fight. People turned and looked at them. They reached an avenue along the river. It was deserted, and the river was deep, slow, silent, almost black.

"Let's go that way," said Agostino after a time. "We've gone far enough." Then he added, "It's a damnable business, and I don't understand it."

"Neither do I," Daniele said in a not very encouraging voice.

"Least of all do I understand the beginning. Why did they take the injured man to your house when their bloody frontier was only a few miles away?"

Daniele had to make an effort to reply.

"Probably they didn't want any questions asked by the Swiss police. The police may already have known about your little exploit."

"Why didn't they put him in a private nursing home?"

"Which private nursing home? How could they trust the staff?"

"But they trusted your family."

Daniele shrugged his shoulders.

"Quite likely they just acted on the spur of the moment," he said. "They probably started out for the frontier, hesitated, changed their minds, turned back, and just stopped at an isolated house."

"And by pure chance it was your house. Do you believe in chance?"

"I no longer believe in anything," Daniele said in an exasperated voice. "I no longer believe in anything, I tell you."

A few yards further on he added:

"Besides, if the man had not been surprised himself at his discovery, why should he have run away? Why shouldn't he have kept me under observation and tried to blow up the whole organization?"

"That may be, but in that case there's another thing I don't understand," Agostino went on.

"If you don't understand, you can at least keep your mouth shut," Daniele snapped at him. "Do you find it so difficult to keep your mouth shut?"

"Don't get angry," Agostino said in a conciliatory tone. "We must try and find the nigger in the woodpile."

"Try yourself!" Daniele replied in exasperation. He added: "We're like two fleas in a pile of oakum. Do you realize that? The most we can do is to try and guess."

"Let's try together. Well, as I was saying, perhaps we were imprudent. Your way of thinking is pretty well known in your neighborhood."

"Yes, in my neighborhood, but not much beyond it. I've never declaimed in the market place."

"Do you trust your neighbors so much? Mind, I only say that as a word of warning for the future."

"In this work I've never trusted anybody, if you want to know. Not even my daughters. I've always done everything myself."

"I know, Daniele, I know. But now I wonder whether we haven't been imprudent. I can't believe that your opinions were unknown to those people."

"It wouldn't be the first time that a secret service has been ignorant about something that was common knowledge. You remember our friend who, after he was put in charge of code work, was no longer able to understand what was printed in the newspapers."

"If that's the way you think, our struggle is just a game of chance."

"Yes, it's a series of gambles. What else can a handful of men do against a dictatorship?"

Agostino refrained from further recriminations. He valued his friendship with Daniele too highly to risk a squabble; without Daniele's friendship everything would collapse. He tried banter.

"So if I'd taken refuge in your house, as we had in mind at first," he said, "I should have had the pleasure of continuing my conversation with your guest."

"Certainly you would," said Daniele. "And, as it's a small house, I should have put you in the same bed."

The river made a big curve. Daniele was sweating and breathless.

"Well, I thought we'd given it, but instead we've taken it," Agostino remarked. "Now what do we do?"

His question fell in the void, and they walked on in silence.

"Let's go back toward the station," Daniele said. "I want to get the next train."

"Stay till tomorrow," said Agostino. "A little rest will do you good; you look dreadful."

"No, I must go back," Daniele said.

"At least have something to eat," Agostino said. "There are trains this afternoon too."

The two men went to an underground *brasserie* lit by neon lighting.

"What a sight we look!" exclaimed Daniele when they passed in front of a mirror.

But in that light the blonde, gold-toothed waitress who came forward and led them to a corner table looked cadaverous too. A banquet that was in full swing gave dignity to the place. The whole of one wall was taken up by a solid row of tables at which a family clan were seated, complete from great-grandfathers and great-grandmothers to great-grandchildren, all seated composedly in hierarchical order in front of mighty platefuls of meat. It was impossible to say whether they were celebrating a wedding or a funeral.

Daniele could not touch his food. He sat leaning against the wall, feeling ill and exhausted.

"Why aren't you eating?" Agostino said reproachfully.

"I've got no appetite," Daniele said. "I'll have a cup of coffee."

"Have you thought of a new base yet on which we could rebuild?"

"I've discussed it with Franz, but haven't decided anything yet. Now I've started wondering whether it's worth while."

"You know that Agnus Dei is known."

"Yes, but for other reasons. He has the good fortune to be thought harmless, because of his religiousness."

"Wouldn't it be better to transfer our base to another part of Switzerland, perhaps the Grisons for a year or two?"

"Yes, it would, but who would look after it? I can't

move again. I've got a farm to look after and a family to keep."

"Of course," said Agostino.

There was another long, embarrassing silence. They seemed condemned to a vicious circle. Meanwhile, the family clan had unanimously and composedly reached the cheese.

"That's why some people say the revolution can be made only by bachelors and paupers," Agostino went on in argumentative tones.

"That's an old idea," said Daniele. "A very old idea. But the bachelors would have to be chaste and poor and have no desire for money, or we'd soon be back where we started, or even further back; and then there'd be the question of what kind of revolution they would be capable of making."

"Don't take everything so literally!" said Agostino, bored by this outburst.

"If you don't want me to, keep your mouth shut," said Daniele.

"I was just talking at random."

"On the contrary, for once you went right to the heart of a question of acute personal concern to us; I mean the question of the real meaning of what we are doing."

"One does what one can."

Daniele was not to be diverted.

"The experiment you mention has already been tried," he went on. "It has been tried by the Church. Monks are both poor and celibate, aren't they? Well, the result has not been very brilliant for the kingdom of heaven on earth." Then he added sarcastically: "By that, I'm not trying to persuade you to abandon celibacy."

Agostino bit his lip to prevent himself from replying.

"Let's change the subject," he suggested patiently, and took an envelope from his pocket. "I've got to give you back the money you gave me last time."

"Haven't you paid the printer?"

"He wouldn't take the money. One bit of good news among all the bad!"

"I'm surprised."

"He told me so as if he were asking me to do him a favor."

"How extraordinary! That old reformist not wanting to be paid? That old fossil? Don't you remember that at first he didn't want even to accept the order? He said it was illegal, risky, contrary to the interests of Swiss neutrality."

"Well, he's changed his mind. Are you sorry?"

"It seems a miracle."

"And that's not the whole story. He wants to talk to some trade-union leaders about our work, in the hope of getting us some money. As you know, some of these unions are rolling in funds."

"I may as well tell you straightaway, I think it's a waste of time."

"But there's no harm in trying. He wouldn't mention our names, of course; he'd act as our guarantor."

"You don't know those trade-union bureaucrats. They're bourgeois to the marrow, particularly those of proletarian origin. The best of them—and note that I say only the best of them, those who still have some sort of ideal—dream of nothing but making the workers middle class. I don't see why they should help us in our struggle."

"That's what you said about the printer."

"Miracles don't keep happening!"

Agostino resented Daniele's persistent undertone of discouragement.

"Well, you're a miracle to us yourself," he said, trying to bring the conversation back to a friendly level.

"That's not true; don't talk nonsense!" Daniele replied.

"If we couldn't count on that kind of miracle, our slavery would be eternal," Agostino said firmly.

"What I wonder is whether we're not mad," Daniele said dryly. "I can't help wondering whether there is any meaning in all this. But now I must go," he went on. "We've talked enough. I'm worried about what may have been happening at home while I've been away."

"I'll come with you to the station."

"No, that would be unwise."

"As for Silvia . . ." Agostino said as they said good-by.

Daniele cut him short.

"That's a matter between you and her," he said.

eleven

Daniele got home late that night. From a distance he saw that the ground-floor lights were on. Perhaps the womenfolk were waiting up for him; but it was not impossible that the police were waiting for him and were keeping a watch on the farm gate. So he decided to approach without being seen. He climbed a fence at the beginning of his farm, and landed up to his knees in the ditch on the other side, and had to take off his boots to empty out the mud and water. It was a cold, dark night. There was a smell of burning in the wind. Where the lake bends beyond Brissago the leaden extent of water was illuminated here and there by streaks of white light from the searchlights of the Italian frontier posts. Daniele advanced cautiously in the dark, carrying his flashlight; he did not switch it on, but kept it ready in case of need. He made a complete circuit of the farm, and approached the house from the side opposite that of the gate. Through a window he saw his wife sitting at a table, sewing under the lamp, and his daughters in the shade near the fireplace. Luisa sat with her head bent on her chest, like a sleepy little sparrow. Filomena's eyes were swollen and red. There was no sign of strangers. Daniele opened the door and silently walked in.

"Heaven be praised!" exclaimed Filomena, putting down her needlework and getting up. Then she added, "Do you want something to eat?"

He did not reply. He seemed to have aged twenty years.

"I'll heat something up for you," said his wife.

He went over to the sink, and took a long drink of water directly from the tap.

"There's a bottle of fresh milk on the table," Filomena went on.

He took no notice. Silvia looked dreadful, but her father did not spare her a glance.

"Have there been any telephone messages, Luisa?" Daniele asked.

He spoke hoarsely, uncertainly, like someone having difficulty with his breathing.

"Someone telephoned from Brissago," the girl replied. "He wanted to let you know that his mother was out of danger."

"There was someone from Ponte Tresa too, if I'm not mistaken," said Filomena.

"Yes, there was," Luisa went on. "He left a message to say that his mother was better. In fact, mothers seem to be doing quite well."

"Not all mothers," Filomena remarked.

At that moment the silence of the night was broken by a piercing animal shriek, like the howl of a dog that has been fatally injured, followed by a prolonged and agitated cackling and fluttering of chickens. Daniele leaped to his feet and dashed out into the garden in the direction of the chicken run. He switched on his flashlight and saw a magnificent fox with its paw caught in the trap. With arched back, frenzied by pain, the hysterical cackling of the chickens, and the sudden blaze of light, it struggled desperately to free the captured limb.

"At last!" Daniele shouted.

He seized an axe from the top of a pile of wood and started striking furiously at the animal, with strength enough to bring down an oak tree. Repeatedly, and with growing violence, he struck at its back, its head, its belly, its paws, and went on striking even after he had reduced it to a bloody pulp.

On his way back to the house Daniele found Luisa standing under the arcade; she had watched the whole thing and was still horrified.

"Come in," her father said. "It's a damp night."

Luisa, walking by his side, took his hand and held it tight.

"Daddy, your hands are burning," she said. "You must be feverish!"

"That'll pass too," her father replied.

"Daddy," the girl asked again, "is what happened

to your papers really serious?"

"Yes, rather serious."

"Is it irreparable?"

"No," her father answered. "As long as you're alive, many things can be remedied."

When they reached the front door and Luisa saw that her father was making straight for the staircase, she said to him:

"Won't you come to the kitchen and have something to eat? I also wanted to tell you that Silvia isn't at all well."

"I only want to sleep," her father replied.

He mounted the stairs with difficulty, stopping several times and leaning against the wall to get his breath. Never in his life had he felt so exhausted; all the accumulated fatigue of the past few days now overwhelmed him at once. When he got to his room he collapsed onto the bed as he was, still with his muddy boots and his hat on, as if crushed by a weight he was no longer able to bear.

Filomena saw the girls to their room and went to him. For a moment she feared the worst. His breath sounded like a death rattle. The hard lines of his face had vanished, leaving visible the anguish and despair he had previously concealed.

"Daniele!" his wife called. "Daniele!"

He could not hear.

"Shall I phone the doctor?" she went on.

Even her efforts to undress him, at any rate partially, and to pull the blankets over him, failed to wake him. She sat beside the bed, not knowing what to do. She felt humiliated at her inability to make up her mind. Thinking about her life, she realized that she had never had to make up her mind. To a stranger the state her husband was in after the strain of the past few days and nights might have seemed natural enough, but for her it was terrifying, for he had never been ill in his life, had never had even an ordinary cold. For Filomena her husband's physical strength and will power constituted the natural order of things, on which the whole stability of the family was based. If both failed, what remained? What was she to do? Should she ask her daughters? It would frighten them and make Silvia's state still worse. Should she send for the doctor? Bringing him from Locarno at this time of night would mean telling him the immediate causes of Daniele's collapse, and she was by no means sure that her husband would welcome this; indeed, it would be only too likely to anger him. Never before had the poor woman had to face the responsibility of a decision of this kind by herself, and never before had she felt so weak, so incapable, so helpless. Reflection only multiplied the dangers. The alarm and anguish she had felt since Signor Cefalù's flight had been kept within bounds by her confidence in Daniele's ability to face and to overcome adversity; but if he, with his courage and exceptional strength, was now reduced to impotence, the last defenses were down, and the plight of the family was beyond repair.

She remained seated beside the bed, her head in her hands, staring into space, stunned. The most trivial things were normally sufficient to cause her to burst into tears, but now her eyes were dry. Tears were useless in her present plight; they were worse than useless, they might imply accepting the situation, accepting the ruin of the family as inevitable. But, though she could not think what to do to avert disaster, she was of no mind to give in to it. For a short time the feeling of her own nullity made her forget Daniele, and, when her attention returned to him, his breathing seemed less labored, more regular and normal. Eventually she convinced herself that there was no immediate danger, and she too went to bed. But she did not feel totally reassured, for in the few hours that remained for sleep she awoke several times to see whether her husband needed anything. At first light, feeling unable to go to sleep again, she got up.

It was a cloudy, cold morning. A gray veil covered the mud-colored water of the lake, the dead-looking trees along the bank and the dismal plain. Luisa was to go back to school that day, after being absent for several days. She had breakfast with her mother, and went upstairs to fetch her books. A little old man, known locally as the greengrocer, appeared at the kitchen door.

"Good morning, madam, good morning!" he said. "Isn't Daniele at home?"

He often used to come to do odd jobs in the garden for Daniele. He was another Italian from Bergamo, and had lived in the Ticino for forty years or more. He had once had a little greengrocer's shop, and, though he had long since failed and was reduced to doing odd jobs for a living, the name had stuck to him.

"My husband is resting," said Filomena.

"Is he unwell?"

"No, I said he was resting."

"I came about the stakes in the garden," the old man explained. "Daniele told me to come last week. He said he wanted me to point the stakes for the tomatoes, beans and peas."

"All right, go ahead," said Filomena. "You'll find the pile of stakes in the usual place."

He was a cheerful old man by nature, but this morning he seemed very depressed. He was in rags, his toes peeped through the cracks in his broken-down shoes and he was shivering with cold.

"I should have come yesterday, but you know what happened," he said.

"I expect you had a hangover," Filomena said. "I've heard you often do."

"It was because of the young man who got drowned," the old man said. "What a thing to happen just before the festival! What? You didn't know? But everyone's talking about it."

"We keep ourselves to ourselves," said Filomena. "We often don't hear things."

Luisa heard what the old man said while coming downstairs.

"Who got drowned?" she asked.

"He was a young man from Locarno," the old man went on. "To judge by his appearance, he must certainly have been a young man of good family. He was seen drowning two days ago, and the body stayed under the water till last night. When it came up again it was a bit swollen, of course, but the face was still fresh and unblemished."

"What happened?" asked Filomena. "How did he get drowned? It's not the bathing season!"

"I'm sorry, I didn't explain properly," the old man said. "It was suicide. He was seen deliberately walking into the water, with his clothes on, in broad daylight."

"A young man?" Luisa exclaimed excitedly. "Was he a student?"

"I can only tell you what I know," the old man said. "Do you remember where the gas station is, about half a mile before the frontier? Well, perhaps you remember that just this side of it there's a path that goes straight down to the bank. Well, the day before yesterday the young man was seen hurrying down it. When he got to the little patch of sand by the waterside he took off his coat, dropped it, made the sign of the cross and walked into the water. At that point it gets deep quickly after about fifty paces. Some little girls saw him, and they started calling out. Apparently he turned and waved to them before he went under. Soon the whole locality was in an uproar. Just a moment."

The old man paused and shut his eyes, the better to remember. His unbuttoned shirt revealed his thin ribs, which showed up like wickerwork.

After a moment he opened his eyes again and went on:

"Let me just go back a bit. I was at the nurseryman's giving a hand with the decorations for an allegorical float that's going to be in the competition at the festival

132

tomorrow. By the way, this year we had an original idea; it's supposed to be secret until tomorrow, but I can tell you. It's a fox holding a dove in its paws under a camellia bush. Well, as I was saying, a neighbor came and told us. We dropped everything and hurried to the bank. The little girls were still there, excited and terrified, pointing out to everybody the spot where the young man went under; and their mothers were there too, imploring them to come home and stop thinking about it, otherwise it might make them ill, and they might get worms because of the fright. The gendarme turned up too, and he took charge of the young man's coat, and he wrote the little girls' names in his notebook, though their mothers objected. 'There's nothing to be done,' the nurseryman said to me, taking me by the sleeve, 'let's get back to work, you know we've got no time to waste.' 'No!' I said to him. 'I'm staying here!' He told me that if I didn't go back with him I'd lose a day's pay. 'Never mind!' I said. The gendarme and I put out a boat and went to the spot the little girls were pointing to. The water was calm, but dirty, and you couldn't see a thing. All the same, we kept at it, going round and round with our eyes fixed on the water until it got dark. 'There's nothing to be done,' said the gendarme. 'He'll come to the surface in forty-eight hours.' Forty-eight hours is a long time for people standing on the bank gazing at the water. During the whole time there was a continual coming and going of officials of every kind, naturally, as he was a young man of good family. As I live nearby, I had to stay there and tell every one of

133

them about it. But it didn't occur to anyone to offer me so much as a *grappa*."

"How dreadful for his poor mother," Filomena said with a sigh.

"He was a young man; do you think he was a student, perhaps?" said Luisa, whose nerves were on edge. "Do they know why he did it?"

"The gendarme told me he left a letter asking his parents' forgiveness," the old man went on. "Forgive me if I don't feel I have the strength to go on. If Daniele were here, he'd certainly offer me a *grappa!*"

"A young man from Locarno?" Luisa went on anxiously. "Don't you know his name?"

"Perhaps it will be in today's papers," the old man said. "Or perhaps not, out of regard for his parents. They're well-to-do people."

"If you don't want to lose another day's school, you'll have to hurry," Filomena said to her daughter.

Luisa took her bicycle from under the portico and went.

"She's growing up well," the greengrocer said admiringly.

"You know where the stakes are," Filomena said. "Don't waste time!"

"I'll need a hook to sharpen them," the old man pointed out.

"You'll find it in the shed," Filomena said. "You know where to look."

"When's Agostino coming back?" the old man asked, before going away. "Lots of people want to know. The place is much less cheerful without him."

"Do you think these are cheerful times?" Filomena replied indignantly.

She went up to the first floor and peeped into the big bedroom. Daniele was still asleep; the noise of the door made him turn over without opening his eyes. Filomena decided that this was a favorable sign, and went back to the kitchen feeling somewhat relieved. As the supply of roasted coffee was getting low, she decided to roast some more. She was just pouring the beans into the roaster when a yell through the window made her heart miss a beat.

"Mummy!"

Luisa appeared in the doorway, livid and distraught. She flung her satchel and a newspaper on the table and dashed into her mother's arms. Some books ended up on the floor.

"What has happened?" her mother asked in terror. "What has happened now?"

"The man who was drowned was Signor Cefalù!" the girl said as soon as she could get her breath back.

"Oh God!" Filomena exclaimed, making the sign of the cross. "It's not possible!"

They remained clasped in each other's arms, weeping and lamenting. The horror with which they had thought of the young Sicilian for the past two days changed suddenly to pity.

"Poor young man!" said Filomena, wiping away her tears. "He didn't deceive us; he was not a bad young man."

Luisa spread the Bellinzona newspaper on the table. The whole of the local news section was devoted to the tragedy. The scene at the lakeside was described in the little girls' own words. The greengrocer was mentioned as one of the volunteers who had spent two days vainly searching for the body. The young man's car had been found on the main road near the gas station. On the front seat he had left his passport, some money and a letter, in which he explained the reason for his act in terms obscure to outsiders. The newspaper quoted some extracts, which it described as "sibylline," under the headline "A Crisis of Conscience?"

"He was not a bad man," Filomena repeated. "He did not want to betray us."

"We must tell Silvia," Luisa said.

"My poor daughter," her mother said. "How she will suffer."

"Yes," said Luisa. "But she'll be able to think of him differently now."

Filomena looked at her daughter with surprise.

"Differently? How?"

"Now she'll be able to think of him with love," Luisa said. "With love and nothing else."

"Yes, you're right," her mother said. "We shall be able to think of him differently too."

"And perhaps what he needs now is that we should remember him with love."

Luisa had said the right thing. Filomena looked gratefully at her younger daughter, and rose with an effort to go up to Silvia's room.

"Don't you think we should tell Daddy too?" Luisa asked.

Filomena came back and sat at the table without answering.

"It concerns him," Luisa went on. "It concerns him very much, though in a different way."

"In a different way," Filomena repeated. "You're quite right, in a different way."

"Shall I go and fetch him?"

"No, wait."

Filomena was staring at the ground, with a grim and mistrustful expression in her eyes.

"We can't hide something from him that concerns him," Luisa insisted. "He'd be right to be angry with us."

"All I'm afraid of is that he might be pleased," Filomena muttered. "That's all I'm afraid of."

"Daddy isn't beastly," Luisa said.

"But he's a fanatic," her mother replied. "I'm afraid he might start laughing with pleasure."

Filomena's expression had hardened.

"If he says one single word of satisfaction, which heaven forbid, if he says one single word . . ." She did not finish the sentence.

Luisa was surprised; she did not recognize her mother's voice.

". . . I don't think Silvia and I would stay in the house," Filomena went on grimly. "I could still find a job as a servant, in spite of my age."

"Mummy, what are you saying?" Luisa exclaimed.

Filomena took no notice of her daughter. Something had snapped inside her, like a string that has been stretched too tight. Luisa looked at her in alarm; then she started picking up the books scattered on the ground and putting them back in her satchel.

"It's late now," she said.

"And you've lost another day's school," her mother remarked.

"I wonder whether it's worth going back to school," Luisa murmured.

"Don't talk nonsense!" said her mother. "You know you've got to get your diploma!"

"Why?" Luisa shrieked in a sudden frenzy. "Do you need a diploma to become a servant?"

Filomena replied with a weary gesture.

"I think we've had enough for today," she said, and rose to go up to Silvia. Luisa remained by the table. On the page of the newspaper next to the story of the suicide there was the detailed program of the Festival of the Camellias.

"Oh God, let it rain tomorrow," Luisa prayed, looking up at the ceiling.

The plaintive wail of the whistle of a locomotive coming from the direction of the frontier sounded in the gray, damp air. Otherwise all that broke the silence was the old man's hacking away at his stakes and the chattering of the sparrows. Luisa took the newspaper and went up to the first floor, determined to confront her father. She went in without knocking, and the sight of the sleeping man took her aback. He looked terrifyingly thin and aged, almost cadaverous. Luisa left the news-

138

paper on the bed and tiptoed out again. On the stairs she started shivering with cold, so she went up to the top floor to fetch a woolen vest from her room. Through the closed doors she could hear her mother's whispers and her sister's quiet sobs. She stood still for a moment, gave up the idea of the woolen vest, and went down to the kitchen again. Some glowing embers were still in the grate, and with a handful of kindling and some logs she got the fire going again.

Not long afterward she heard the heavy footsteps she was waiting for with dread and apprehension. Daniele came heavily downstairs and stopped in the kitchen doorway.

"I've read the news," he said.

Luisa, staring into the fire, waited in trepidation for what was to follow.

"I'm sorry about the young man," her father went on slowly. "He wasn't a bad young man."

Luisa was more moved by his hoarse voice, which was full of compassion, than by what he said.

"Come over by the fire," she said without turning her head, so that he should not see her tears. "I'll get you some coffee."

Daniele came and sat by the fire and held out his hands to warm them.

"How is Silvia?" he asked.

"She's crying," Luisa replied, wiping her eyes. "Tears don't waken the dead, but what else can one do?"

"While you're getting the coffee," Daniele said, "I'll go up and see her for a moment."

About the Author

IGNAZIO SILONE was born in the Italian town of Pescina in the Abruzzi in 1900. His father was a small landowner, his mother a weaver. He received his early schooling in Pescina and then studied for the priesthood in Catholic institutions in various Italian towns.

As a young man Mr. Silone was involved in the anti-war movement and, after Mussolini's *coup d'état,* in the Communist underground, fighting the Fascist regime. Between 1928 and 1944 he lived in exile in Switzerland, where, in 1940, he organized a network of Socialist underground resistance groups against the Fascists. He returned to Italy and became a leader in the Italian Socialist Party from 1944 to 1948, after which he worked for two years to unite the anti-Communist Socialist elements in the country. Since 1950 Mr. Silone has not been associated with any political group.

Some of Mr. Silone's most famous books were written during his years of exile. They include the novels *Fontamara* and *Bread and Wine. The Secret of Luca,* his most recent novel, was published with impressive critical acclaim in 1958. He is also the author of *The School for Dictators,* a play entitled *And He Hid Himself,* and a chapter in *The God That Failed,* which describes his conversion from Communism.

Set in Bodoni Book
Format by Jacqueline Wilsdon
Manufactured by The Haddon Craftsmen, Inc.
Published by Harper & Brothers, New York